Dear Drama

Dear Drama

Braya Spice

www.urbanbooks.net

Urban Books, LLC
78 East Industry Court
Deer Park, NY 11729

ISBN 13: 978-1-60162-341-6
ISBN 10: 1-60162-341-0

First Trade Paperback Printing April 2012
Printed in the United States of America

10 9 8 7 6 5 4 3 2 1

Distributed by Kensington Publishing Corp.
Submit Wholesale Orders to:
Kensington Publishing Corp.
C/O Penguin Group (USA) Inc.
Attention: Order Processing
405 Murray Hill Parkway
East Rutherford, NJ 07073-2316
Phone: 1-800-526-0275
Fax: 1-800-227-9604

Dedication

This novel is dedicated to my single-parent sisters. The road for us has always been tough. Still, we make a way and continue to pull through. Love is on the horizon. . . .

Acknowledgments

Braya Spice is in the building! As you all know, I also write as Karen Williams.

My novels, *Harlem On Lock, The People Vs. Cashmere, Dirty to the Grave,* and *Thug in Me;* my short story collection, *Aphrodisiacs: Erotic Short Stories;* and the anthologies that I have contributed stories to, *Around the Way Girls 7* and *Even Sinners Have Souls Too,* have all been urban fiction. *Dear Drama* is my first contemporary work!

I hope you enjoy this story, and I hope it gives a voice to all the women out there that have been on this quest for love, have made mistakes, have been through the ringer and back, and still truly want to experience wholesome, unconditional love. Ladies, know that you don't have to allow yourself to be mistreated, be with a piece of a man, or trade one bad man in for another to have someone. Despite the fears you may have about not finding someone to love you, know there is no need at all to settle. And all that you aspire to have, you shall have. Trust. ☺

I want to thank my beautiful children, Adara and Bralynn. It is so funny that since my son was born, I have written three books. And this is with my son being on my hip! Honestly! As long as he has his dinosaurs and can watch *Dino Dan,* he allows his mommy to write. Adara, since her conception, hasn't been a problem and still, to this day, inspires me to be all that I am.

Acknowledgments

Sending love to my sister "Crystal" and my mother.

Hey to my nieces, Mikayla and Maydison; my nephews Omari and Jeff Jr.; my cousins Donnie, Jabrez, Devin, and Mu-Mu; and my goddaughter La'naya. Hey to Tammy, Shauntae, Ray, Eric, Christina, and Terry.

Thanks to my friends Sheryl, Roxetta, Lenzie, Christina, Kimberly, Linda, Tracy, Christina, Talamontes, Pam, Carla, Sewiaa, Ronisha RIP, Tina, Shumeka, Valerie Hoyt, Tara, Pearlean, Maxine, Dena, Barbara, Henrietta, Candis, VI, Phillipo, Latonya, Leigh and Vanilla, Yvonne Gayner, Sandra V, Sandra T, Ivy, Daphne and Lydia, Mrs. Pope, Rob, Tiffany and Trudy.

Big ups to all my author buddies, Mondell Pope, Aleta Williams, Terra Little, Terry L. Wroten, and Angel Williams. Rainne Grant, you inspire me! Hey Netta!

Thanks to Carl and Natalie! Natalie, I know your job is demanding, and I truly appreciate all the hard work that you do. I'm 100 percent sincere when I say that. Thanks for believing in me, Carl, to the extent that you took a gamble on this book! Thanks Rosemary! Thanks to my editor, Kevin Dwyer. I love, love, love you to pieces! ☺

Dear Drama is here. . . . Enjoy!

Prologue

January 2007

"You gonna put this fucking ring on!"

I could not fucking breathe.

I stared at Greg as spit flew from his mouth and his hands were wrapped around my throat. As his hold tightened, I started to gag and choke. Then lines of snot flew from my nose. But that crazy muthafucka would not stop choking me.

My hands went to cover his hands.

My eyes pleaded. I hoped he would see the begging and feel sorry for hurting me, and he would stop.

He released my neck and looked me in my eyes like he had won. "You gonna wear this shit or not?"

It was an engagement ring. This fool didn't get it. How many more times could I let him punch me in the mouth or bash my head into a wall in front of our daughter? My hearing in my right ear was already fucked up, and I was wearing a tooth implant in the front of my mouth. I had left his ass for a reason, and now he thought he was going to persuade me to come back to him with a punk-ass engagement ring? I had too much to lose. A little girl that was his, Sierra. And I refused to let her see her mom get her ass whipped by her father again.

Enough was fucking enough. That was why I had left his ass like a thief in the night. And now he had found me. . . .

He slapped me to get my attention. Despite being slapped numerous times by him, I had never gotten used to the pain. It was paralyzing and brought heat to whatever spot he hit.

I blinked and stared at the shiny engagement ring in front of me. It had my birthstone in the middle, with diamonds around it. Pretty. But fuck that. I shook my head, indicating no. I refused. I was not marrying him. I deserved to be happy. I was a good person, and I took good care of our daughter and didn't treat people bad. In fact, I had been the perfect girlfriend to Greg, but he had still treated me bad. I was ready to move on and see what a healthy, wholesome relationship felt like. I knew Greg could never give me that, 'cause if he could, he would have done it already. He was far too violent and far too jealous to be anything other than what he was. Two years with him had shown me that. If you could beat the mother of your child in front of your child, then you were really a low person. A person I wanted to do without.

He punched me in the side of my head and went back to choking me. And mind you, this was all going on while our two-year-old daughter stood in front of us, horrified, and watched.

Alarm hit me. What if this was it? He had always said that he would kill me if I were to leave him. What if he ended my life this night because I refused to go back to him and agree to marry him? I knew I could not let that happen. If there was ever a time to fight, now was it. My daughter needed me. I swung at him with my fist, refusing to let him take me out.

His hands released my neck so he could dodge my hits and grip me by my hair.

I winced in pain. "Sierra! Code ten," I yelled.

She dashed away, snatched the cordless phone off the end table. She knew code ten was her cue to dial 911. I had already prepped her that if her dad found us, this was what we would have to do.

When Greg saw her with the phone in her hand, he let me go. "Sierra, put the phone down, baby. Daddy got warrants. You don't want me to go back to jail, do you?"

She dialed the three numbers quickly, and then she put her tiny middle finger in the air and ran out of the living room to our hallway.

Greg's eyes widened.

If I weren't in pain, I would have laughed.

With a kick to my body, he dashed out of the house so he could be gone before the cops could get there.

I grimaced at the pain I was feeling, and hoped he didn't leave any more bruises. But touching my face told me my right cheek, where he slapped me, was swollen.

That was when I heard sniffles coming from the hallway of our studio apartment. I grimaced again and slowly stood. I walked in the hallway, to find Sierra tucked in the corner, crying.

"Awww. It's okay, baby."

I scooped her into my arms and hugged her, knowing I had made the right decision by leaving that crazy muthafucka. And I sighed, because I knew I would have to move again.

Chapter 1

Before I start running over my life any further, let me introduce myself. My name is Allure Jones. I'm about to be twenty-one. I have slanted eyes, could pass for a mix of Chinese and black if I were a little lighter, but I'm not. I have brown skin. I have shoulder-length hair but wear braids 90 percent of the time, because I have a lot on my plate and don't have time to be constantly going to my older sister's beauty salon to get my hair done, although when I do, my hair stay looking fly. I have nice teeth for someone who used to have a massive overbite, and my mama didn't take the time to get me braces, because she was too busy trying to raise my sister, I, and my two brothers—(who both live in Spokane, Washington)—alone. I reside in Long Beach, CA.

I have full lips, which I am just now embracing, because before I was constantly made fun of for having full lips and was even called a monkey when I was a kid. I have a splash of beauty marks on my face and body that I inherited from my grandmother. Now the body . . . big breasts, D cups to be exact; a small, slight curve, which I call my ass; pretty calves. That about describes me. My older sister, who is twenty-four, is identical to me, except she is only five-one and her hairstyles, from weaves to lace fronts, change with the weather.

I have been told I am pretty, cute, sexy, and even fine. I have a beautiful baby girl named Sierra and a crazy-ass baby daddy named Greg. I gave him my virginity, he in turn got me knocked up, and a few months after my daughter was born. He gave me a very unpleasant surprise: chlamydia. And more ass whippings than Ike gave Tina. I managed to break free of his crazy ass and was now trying to make it on my own, if I could, which was hard as hell. We managed to elude him, keep him from figuring out where were for staying, for two months, but he found out. It was like he was the FBI. After the incident where he tried to strangle me, Sierra and I packed our shit and moved again.

It wasn't the home of my dreams. But it sure as hell was better than where I had come from as a kid. It didn't have any rats or roaches. Sierra could have her own room, due to my Section 8 voucher, and she had a yard to play in. The only problem was that it was smack-dab in the hood, on the eastside Long Beach on Magnolia and Pacific Coast Highway. But, when you were living on minimum wage and financial aid, it was the best that you could do. And I, indeed, was doing my best. I was going to college full-time at Long Beach City College and I, worked in their child development center as a child care worker about twenty-five hours a week. It wasn't a lot of hours or money, but the schedule allowed me to study and go to class and not neglect Sierra. The job also gave me the opportunity to get the hell off of welfare before I became dependent on that shit. But I never had much luck getting Greg to give me child support. He would quit his job just so he didn't have to pay me, and he worked under the table because he was just trifling. I had hoped my hard work in college would eventually land me a position teaching high school English. That was my goal.

I smiled when the phone rang. I rushed to the living room to answer it.

When a male's voice said hello, I recognized it as Greg's. I hadn't heard from him since the day he tried to strangle me and tear my arm from my socket. One month had passed since then, marking our third month of separation.

"Hey," I said dryly. I started to ask him how he got my number, but I figured he probably called 411. I couldn't afford to get it blocked. And it made no sense to avoid him any longer, anyway. He was, after all, Sierra's father, and I had to deal with him. I just wished he would accept that it was over between us and would act like he had some sense.

Over the two years of our relationship, he not only cheated on me with numerous women, but also beat the hell out of me for things even he couldn't explain. If I went outside our apartment in a dress he claimed was too little, smack! Or if I argued back at him when he accused me of sleeping around and called me every bad word known to mankind, smack! Sometimes I wondered how I got away from his crazy ass alive. He threatened to kill me so many times, it got to the point where I was just waiting for it to happen. And that day he showed up at my apartment two months before, I thought he was going to kill me.

His gruff voice brought me back to the present. "Since I figured it's your birthday, I thought I'd take Si Si for the whole week and give you a break."

I hesitated. I didn't feel comfortable dealing with Greg since our leaving him, because I didn't know what he would do next. But at the same time I did not want to keep him from his daughter. I went back and forth with myself, not knowing the proper choice to make.

"Listen, I know I fucked up in the past and I fucked off our relationship, and I accept that you don't want me back. But I'm not fucking off my kid. I love you and

Sierra, and now I'm going to focus on being the best father I can be to her and help take some of the stress off of you."

"Greg, the last time you popped up at my house, you put your hands on me."

"And I'm sorry about that. Allure, listen. That kind of shit is wrong, and if I don't learn to control my temper, I'm going to end up in jail for really hurting someone. You have my word. I'm done with that. I promise you."

He sounded sincere, but I had learned to question his words because they were not always sincere. He had promised me time and time again that he would keep his hands to himself and stop disrespecting me, but he always reneged. Still, I wanted Sierra to have her father in her life. I had lost mine when I was six in a bus accident. So I never knew what it was like to have a father. It had to be different for my daughter. But I didn't want Greg to know where I lived, by any means, so coming to my house was out. I figured out a safer alternative.

"Okay. I'll drop her off at your mother's house." I almost expected him to argue. But it was his mother's house or nothing. He wasn't going to get another chance to act stupid in my home.

"That's fair enough. I know I acted a—"

I cut him off. "What time do you want me to drop her off?"

"Is ten o'clock okay?"

"Yeah."

"Allure?"

"What?" I snapped.

"I love you."

I hung up before I made a smart comment that would have us arguing. I no longer loved Greg. I no longer had the desire to be with him. He had done too much to me for me to feel that sentiment toward him. Part of me hated him. Another part feared him. Which was why I hung up before ugly things spilled from my mouth.

Next thing I knew, I was wearing my version of Beyoncé's "freakum" dress, which was pink and tight fitting, and backing my ass up on the dance floor to Kanye West's "Good Life." I was more tipsy than a little bit, and next to me, taking it all the way down, was my sister, Crystal, who had hooked up my hair and makeup, and my friend Creole, who was on the stage with her head tossed back and her thonged ass being exposed. Kendra had passed on coming.

"You look like you having fun over there!" my sister said while doing the two-step.

I laughed, closed my eyes, and took my body all the way to the floor and slowly brought it up. I didn't have to hold myself back from anything any damn more. I didn't have to stay cooped up in the house while my friends enjoyed their early twenties. I was fucking free. I wasn't Greg's punching bag anymore. I didn't have to hear him curse at me or call me out of my name.

A dude slipped into our circle and curled an arm around my waist so I was grinding on him. He was rubbing his hands up and down my waist and calling me sexy. I was having a ball, and I would have continued dancing if I didn't damn near scream when I caught sight of Poo. That was Greg's boy. He was right across from me, freaking on a chick, and yeah, his hands were all over her but his eyes were all over me. His look was clear. It said, "I'm going to tell."

Now, I knew I wasn't with Greg anymore, so I was doing no wrong and had no reason to trip, but there was something about the way he was looking at me and something about how he slipped away from the girl he was dancing with. Then he was on a cell phone, which had me scared. I knew if he were to call Greg, Greg would be here with quickness. So I was now no longer feeling any confidence, and my steps were now awkward and stiff. I couldn't help but feel apprehension. Which pissed me off, because I shouldn't have to feel this way. I was single, trying to have a good time! I wasn't neglecting my child. I handled my business in school and at work, yet the problems were still present because of Greg.

The next thing I knew, Poo was walking up to me. He paused one feet away, looked at me, smirked, and shook his head. Then he twisted the hat on his head. The dude dancing with me moved in closer on me and was gripping my hips. Poo shook his head one more time and walked away. When the song ended, I hugged the guy and rushed away.

From that point on I couldn't seem to break away from Poo's ass, either. Every song I danced to, alone or with a guy, was under his eyes, and the shit made me so uncomfortable, I could no longer enjoy myself. At one point he was even talking on his cell phone as I danced with a guy, and I was scared he was talking to Greg. I was so focused on him and what he was saying that I ended up tripping into the girl behind me.

"Watch where the fuck you going," she snarled in my ear.

"Shut up, bitch," I said, calmly walking away.

She continued to wolf, but I ignored her and walked off the floor.

My sister followed after me. "Where you going?"

"Can we go now?" I didn't want to tell her why, so I lied. "I'm kinda hungry."

"Okay, we can go to Denny's and get something."

I led the way because I wanted to get the hell out of there just in case Greg popped up in and started some shit. 'Cause if he did pop up, it would be some shit. I knew that for sure.

"Damn, Allure, slow down. Damn, you act like you starving! And we were having fun," Creole yelled.

I instantly felt bad for stopping short our fun because of the possibility of an encounter with Greg. But I laughed nervously and didn't slow down until I was in my sister's Pathfinder. They hopped in and the car started, and then, and only then, was I able to breathe right.

So we escaped to Denny's and had breakfast there. I thought back to all the fun I was having before I saw Poo, and was disappointed that we had to cut it short, but I needed no drama from Greg.

Although I had had a good time at the club before seeing Poo, I couldn't see myself in there every weekend. Still, I had a wad of phone numbers, which I stuffed in my purse as my sister's truck pulled up to my apartment.

"Bye!" I told Crystal and Creole. My sister was going to drop Creole off at home.

They both chorused, "Bye."

I hopped out of the truck and walked toward my apartment gate. I pulled my key to the gate out of my purse then pulled out my keys to get into the house. I opened the gate and walked through it. My smile dropped as I got closer to my apartment. I saw a figure sitting on my porch.

Shit.

Although it was dark, my eyes were able to make out Greg's figure. When I saw it was him, I jumped and prayed to God my sister would not drive away until she saw I had made it into my apartment.

He stood calmly and flicked his cigarette on the grass. "You look like a fucking rat."

"It would be a waste of time to ask how you found me, wouldn't it?" I asked calmly. But inside I wasn't calm. This bastard should get a job being a private investigator. Or a bounty hunter. I was filled with fear and dread, because I liked my place and did not want to have to move again.

He chuckled. "Hey, you know me."

"Where's Sierra?"

"My mom's." He eyed me up and down.

I glanced back to see if my sister and Creole were still parked there. Luckily, they were. Since Greg had moved underneath a tree, their view of him was probably blocked. They parked on the other side of the street and probably could see only me. I didn't know whether to run or scream; I was too scared to do anything, so I stood there, frozen.

"Yeah, Poo told me what's up, but I had to see the shit for myself. Shot up to the club. Your ashy black ass was a ghost. What makes you think you can run the streets, looking and acting like a ho? I should haul your slutty ass to Watts and let them project niggas run a train on you. But I don't want to funk up my car with that stank box of yours."

I ignored his insults. I wanted to stay calm. I didn't need any commotion at three o'clock in the morning. I didn't want my neighbors to hear us arguing. "I didn't invite you to my house, so go home and don't come back," I said.

Before I could say anything else, Greg stepped away from the tree and raised a hand.

I screamed and backed up a little, knowing he was going to hit me.

"Shut up!" He slapped me across my face with all his might. I held the side of my face as the pain rushed to it. I cowered, hoping that would stop him, but he instead landed a punch to my mouth.

"Oh, hell no!" someone yelled.

I glanced up and saw my sister hop over the fence of my apartment and Creole run through the gate in a flash.

Praise God, I thought.

They both lunged at Greg, pounding him with their fists. I started attacking him also. I slapped him, kicked him, and spit in his face as Creole and Crystal continued pummeling him. Crystal had even snatched off one of her heels and was beating him over the head with it.

"How you like it?" she raged.

He swung blindly and yelled, "You fucking bitches!"

"Ho-ass nigga!" Crystal yelled, pounding him in his back.

We continued to hit him until he knocked Crystal down and escaped to a spot a few feet away from us.

All of us were breathing deeply.

"If I had my hammer, I'd blow all y'all bitches' heads off!" he threatened.

By now all my neighbors had come out of their apartments to watch. I stood there, embarrassed, with my head down. All the times in the past when Greg had assaulted me, my neighbors had come outside to watch but had never helped. Then they had looked down and told me how dumb I was for staying with this man. I had wanted to escape all of that drama. And I had, but now I was back there, looking like an idiot again in front of my new neighbors.

"You just made a terrorist threat," Crystal pointed out, standing to her feet.

Creole laughed loudly. "Yeah, you bitch ass!"

This all made him angrier. He never took his eyes off of me, though. His face held an evil scowl. Silently, he was telling me that if it weren't for my sister and Creole, I'd be on a stretcher right about now. "Bitch," he muttered. Then he turned to walk away.

"Stay the fuck away from my sister," Crystal warned.

He flicked her off and kept walking.

"That muthafucka! We were wondering what was taking you so long to go into your place. Then we saw someone come out of the shadows like the night stalker, and you screamed. We figured it had to be Greg's crazy ass," Creole said.

Crystal turned to me, lifted my chin with her hand, and examined my face. I heard her sigh as her eyes passed over my cheek that was swollen and my bottom lip, which was busted. There was blood gushing out.

I used the bottom of my shirt to wipe some of it away. My whole mouth burned. But I was used to the feeling. I was just glad he didn't knock any of my teeth out.

"I hate that bastard," she whispered.

One of my neighbors must have called the police, because the next thing we knew, their sirens were blaring and they were pulling up on my street.

Chapter 2

March 2008

It was a Saturday. I was reliving all the good about my birthday from the year before and trying to block out the bad. Now I was twenty-two, and Sierra was three.

Although I had the time of my life on my birthday the year before, I chose not to do the nightclub thing this year so I could have enough money to take Sierra to Disneyland for her third birthday. She had a ball. Instead, I ordered a pizza and hung out with Kendra. See, I didn't have too many friends, just her, my friend Creole. I mean, I had a few associates, but these two were my dear friends.

I had known Creole since I was thirteen. She was short like my sister, five-one, and talked more shit than a little bit. She was high yellow, with short, curly reddish hair and a curvy frame to die for. Kendra was dark skinned, had a very pretty face, with jet-black hair that hung down her back. She was more plus sized. I met Kendra at school when I was nineteen, when I was going through all my bullshit with Greg. She was really there for me when I needed her. She never gave me the lines others did, like, "Girl, you should leave his ass. You stupid," or my personal favorite, "If I was you, I would . . ." It didn't take me long to figure out that those same women who said those things were sometimes in worse situations than mine—which was hard to imagine—and stayed. Yet they were quick to judge my situation. Bitches like them were so fucking judgmental. You said, "My baby is late. He's usually home by nine. It's nine fifteen." They said, "Girl, you know he's fucking around!" But let them come home and find a woman in their bed. All the rules changed. "I found this girl in my bed, but my man said he don't know how she got there. Do you think he's cheating on me?" *Yes! Duh, bitch!* Your friends could be your worst critics. The shit they told you just didn't, for some reason, apply to them. And you had to be careful what advice you took from your friends. It could often be biased, based on their own misery. They were alone, so they wanted you to be alone. That was why I didn't deal with too many broads. But Creole and Kendra . . . they were just different. They were my road dawgs. And neither were judgmental.

Both had their own beliefs on things. Kendra: "Love is possible." Creole: "Fuck love." Kendra: "You'll find that dream man one day." Creole: "Fuck that. Get in his pockets." But you needed two completely different friends that provided a balance to your perspective.

Kendra was curled on the love seat in my apartment, while I stretched out on the floor. Both of us held our stomach after all the pizza we had just grubbed on with our greedy asses.

"Do you realize that you have been alone for over a year?" she asked me out of the blue.

"'Cause that crazy bastard Greg almost made me want to turn gay."

My friend nodded and said, "How you feel now?"

"What you think? I'm ready to get loved on. It's a fucking Sahara down there. But I want something serious. No bullshit. You already know how I do things."

"But I'll be honest. Shit is worse now for single women than ever, and especially if you a black woman, the pickings are so fucking slim. The bottom line is this. They don't want us. It used to be that you may have had a hard time getting a man to marry you. Now you have a hard time getting a man just to commit to you. 'Cause all the niggas got women at home already."

That wasn't the first time I had heard that. I remembered watching a special on ABC and seeing so many educated black women in their thirties who were still not married. I didn't want that to be me. After I finished college and got the career that I wanted, I wanted to get married and have more pretty babies like Sierra.

"You heard from your crazy-ass baby's daddy?" Kendra asked.

"Let's not discuss him," I pleaded.

Greg had been arrested the night of my twenty-first birthday. It was obvious from looking at my face that he had attacked me. Crystal also threw in that he had made a terrorist threat against all three of us. They gave him sixteen months in jail, but he had to serve only half of that. Once he got out, the courts made him take domestic violence, anger management, and parenting classes. Luckily, he wasn't allowed to see Sierra until he completed them. According to his mother, he was really doing well in them. I was just happy he wasn't around to harass me. And deep down, I hoped this would help him. I did, after all, want Greg to be a part of Sierra's life, just not the way he was. I mean, the way I felt about us getting back together wasn't going to change. I wanted no parts of him for me. But I wanted him to be a real father to Sierra. Even if he wasn't paying child support.

While he was in jail, he wrote letters to Sierra and me every week. In the letters, he claimed that he had changed and that he realized how wrong he was. He even begged me for another chance. I never replied. I just read the letters addressed to Sierra to her and threw the ones he wrote me in the trash. There was no way in hell I was going back to him. He had robbed me of two years of my life. Greg wasn't getting any more of my life to ruin.

I was trying to live my life like it was golden. My first step was to get me some and a man. It was not an easy task.

I didn't have a problem meeting guys. I was, after all, friends with a damn man magnet: Creole. But let's just say the men Creole dated weren't my type at all. I mean, our agendas, Creole and I, were way too different. That was because Creole was different. Creole would tell you in a minute: "I don't give a damn how the nigga look. He don't even have to have all his limbs, but the dollars better be long, or I'm not fucking with you. If the motherfucker missing both arms, he better damn well know how to maneuver the hell out an Escalade with his shoulders!"

While I was seeking someone to love me, I made the bad choice of having Creole hook me up with someone. His name was Ruju. He was African and looked like he was part alien, because he was that damn ugly. My first instinct told me to do an about-face back into my apartment when I greeted him at my door. He was brown skinned, with long dreads that smelled like moldy bread. He was missing four bottom teeth and was blind in his right eye, and the left was bloodshot red. He had stitches in his nose, and his nostrils were super huge. I tried look past all that and zoom in on his great personality, but he didn't have one. His accent was so thick, I could barely understand him. So I nodded and smiled the whole way to the restaurant.

The dishes we ordered at the restaurant, I couldn't pronounce. They consisted of goat and something that looked thick as grits and was covered in a dark sauce. I passed on the fare and instead munched on the fried plantains. He was too busy sopping up the grits and the bloody-looking gravy to notice. And I would say the date was going pretty well until Ruju got a little frisky and copped a feel under the table with his greasy, slobbery hands, which he had just licked.

I narrowed my eyes and gave him a look that said, "Don't fuck with me." The snarling of my lips meant this was his last and only warning. It seemed that he heeded it as I sipped my water.

However, when the waitress brought the check, he took the diversion as an opportunity to shove his hands underneath my skirt and tried to stick a finger in my panties.

Without much reservation, I took my fork and stabbed his leg with it. "What in the fuck is wrong with you?"

He leaped back and howled in pain.

I rose from the table with my purse and stalked angrily to the door as he chased after me.

"I'm sorry, *babbe!* I meant no harm. You're just so fine." He rubbed the spot on his thigh where I had poked him. Unfortunately, I had drawn no blood.

"Pay the bill so you can take me home, clown," I barked and marched outside to his car.

"I'm so, so very sorry. I want to take you to the movies and shopping on Sunday. Can I, Adure?"

"It's Allure."

"Sorry, Abure?"

I ignored him. That was probably the closest he would get to pronouncing my name right.

I didn't listen to any more of his jabber. I just concentrated on the tongue-lashing I was going to give Creole for fixing me up with this ugly bastard.

Once he pulled up to my street, I unsnapped my seat belt and grabbed my purse. I flashed him another evil look and reached for the door handle. I opened the door but froze when I felt something on one of my breasts. My eyes dropped instantly to a black, ashy-ass hand.

"Muthafucka, I said don't touch me!" I grabbed his container of now lukewarm food and beat him over the head with it. Goat meat, gravy, and grits went everywhere. I shook my head, exited his car, and slammed the door as hard as I could. "Get your ass out of here, you fucking foreigner!" And he did.

After him, I refused to let Creole set me up with anyone else. I found men on my own.

I went from him to a mailman who invited me over for dinner. Then his three-hundred-pound wife showed up and whipped my ass. Then I met a stalker named Mike who worked for 411, and after we had one, *one,* phone conversation, the next thing I knew this fool showed up at my door, with a sleeping bag and a stuffed pillowcase with clothes threatening to spill from it, and thought he was going to move in! When I cursed his ass out for showing up at my house, he sucked his teeth and mumbled, "I'll go to my other bitch." He swung his sleeping bag and pillowcase over his shoulder and walked away. Now every time I call 411, I can never get the number I need, because I always get hung up on. I guess he blackballed my number. Let's just say that these experiences left me a little traumatized, well, that and dealing with my run-ins with Greg.

***

I was still willing to give dating another try. After the disaster dates I met this dude. His nickname was Mc-Coy. I met him when I was outside washing my car. He said he was mesmerized by my legs.

While I dried off my car, he just leaned against his and watched me the whole time, until finally I snapped, "You want something?"

He chuckled. He was still in his work uniform, which was a pair of scrubs. He was cute, tall, with a nice body. But that didn't mean shit. Greg was cute, but on the inside he was revolting. The mailman was cute and Mike was fine, but both were losers. I had learned not to rely just on a person's looks.

"Yeah, I want something."

"Oh yeah, and what's that? 'Cause what you want just might be on Figueroa or Compton Boulevard. But best believe it won't be here."

The mail lady, Etta, was shoveling mail in our slot and cracked up laughing at what I said. She was the only mail person I knew that came so late. It could be eight in the evening, and here comes her ass, delivering the mail or taking a break and sitting on my porch steps. Every time I saw her, she had a cigarette hanging from her mouth.

He cracked up laughing, too, like what I said got him so tickled. "Sexy, I don't mess with hoes. But I'll spoil the hell out of a lady." He had dimples and a bashful smile. "You know damn well what to expect when you come out here looking like that."

I blushed now. I was a sucka for a compliment. But I quickly placed my frown back on my face. "Are you gonna answer my question?"

He crossed his arms underneath his chest. "Yeah. I'm waitin' around to see who own those legs."

I laughed. He was funny.

And a week later we were at the movies. It felt nice to be out on a date. I felt . . . of the world. And he paid too. I was just hoping for the best. I had a box of nachos, a Cinnabon pretzel, and a cherry Slurpee, and he wasn't trying to feel me up, either, like the African guy.

"You okay?" he asked me as the previews came on.

I smiled, super happy we made it in time for the previews. I hated to miss the previews. "Yeah, I'm fine."

"Good." He slipped his hand in mine. That was cool. A couple seconds later I know I wasn't crazy when I felt someone else grab my other hand.

What the hell?

I snapped my head to the right, because McCoy was on my left, and met the red, hate-filled eyes of Greg.

Goddamn!

I pulled my hand away, and dread instantly filled me. "Greg, what are you doing here?" I screeched, exploding.

"What you mean, what I'm doing here? What the fuck you doing here?"

I took a deep breath as McCoy leaned over me and glared at Greg. "What the fuck is this?" he demanded.

"Who the fuck you cursing at?" Greg demanded.

"Greg, stop!"

He ignored Greg. "Allure, who is this?"

"He's my baby's daddy!"

"What?" McCoy slid his hand from mine.

"No, McCoy, don't." I turned to Greg and whispered, "Greg, you better get the hell away." Inside my heart was pounding, because I didn't know what he would do. True, he had been to all those classes, which seemed to have mellowed him out somewhat. Since he had been home, he hadn't threatened me again or popped up at my place unannounced, but this was the first time he had seen me with another man on a date. My heart sped up, and I was slightly embarrassed, but I tried to keep a straight face to show Greg I really would call his PO.

He gave me a hateful look and got up. He went to the row right behind me and sat down, making it impossible for me to enjoy my date or the movie. I knew McCoy felt the same way. Because he kept shaking his head and shifting in his seat. He refused to talk to me, even when I asked him if he was enjoying the movie, and Greg crunching on his popcorn set my nerves on edge to the point that I wanted to scream. I understood McCoy's anger, though. What if he brought me to the movies and his baby mother showed up? But then again, since I knew what it was like to have a crazy ex, maybe I would have understood. Who knows?

But those were two very uncomfortable hours. I wanted to curse at Greg and tell him to get the fuck away from us, but I didn't want to make a scene and possibly set Greg off. So I painfully rode those two hours out. But inside I was pissed. Greg needed to accept that I had moved on and we were not going to get back together, and that I was going to date, kiss and, yes, have sex with other men. He would have to.

And even though I liked McCoy, after our first date, he never called me again. I couldn't say that I didn't know why.

Chapter 3

They say you'll find the one when you least expect it. But what if you least expect it and you find a real asshole? That's how I describe how I met Lavante. It was a week after my date with McCoy. I was at the grocery store, zooming down one aisle, trying to get some food on my lunch break, when I saw him coming the opposite way. I paid him no mind at first. I just scanned the shelf for the fruit snacks Sierra loved. I did, however, catch him casting looks my way. He was dressed in an orange construction suit. Another man dressed like him, but slightly overweight and dark skinned, walked with him. Both had their name on their uniform. The one checking me out was named Lavante, and the other one was named Cedric. He stared my way and chuckled. Once I found the item I needed, I rushed to check out so I could drop the food at home and rush back to work. I didn't expect him to follow me out to my car.

"You forgot something," he informed me with a quick smile.

"I did?"

"Yeah. My number."

I refrained from rolling my eyes at his corny come-on line.

"How are you?"

"I'm good, and you?"

"If I can take you to dinner sometime soon . . . fucking great."

I chuckled. "What's your name, anyway?"

"Lavante." He shook my hand.

"Well, my name is Allure, and can you slow down a little?"

He chuckled. "I'm sorry. I see a pretty girl and I go crazy. Well, would you mind if we exchanged numbers, and we can discuss going out to dinner?"

"That's fine. That I can do." Upon closer inspection I noted he looked a lot older than me, maybe in his late thirties or early forties. With brown skin, a closely shaven head, and a thin mustache over his medium-sized lips. He had a defined body, which was very apparent in his uniform. I didn't mean to be disrespectful and look between his legs, but damn! He had a big bulge there.

We exchanged numbers. He lingered a little longer, helping me load my food in my car. Then he retreated back into the store.

It turned out that Lavante did call the following day.

"Hi. How have you been?" I asked him after receiving his warm greeting.

He was a cool conversationalist. He asked me various questions about my likes information reminded me of how long it had really been since I had dated a guy. Far too long. Lavante seemed interesting enough. He was forty-one, had worked in construction for over ten years, and had no kids. I didn't care if he did, anyway, because I had a child, but he had none.

We talked for a total of two weeks. The fact that I was able to intrigue a man nearly twice my age made me feel a little wiser than my young years. I felt sophisticated.

"What are your plans today?" Lavante asked me after
we were chatting for a good twenty minutes. I found
out he was from Louisiana and he was forty–one years
old and had been single for a year.

"I don't have any," I said.

It was a Saturday. My only option was to go to the
mall and spend money I didn't have, and then spend
the rest of the weekend regretting it.

"I was wondering if I could see you today. Maybe we
could go to lunch and continue our intriguing conversations, pretty lady."

I blushed. He thought I was intriguing? *Wow*. "Yeah,
that would be okay." I tried to keep the excitement out
of my voice.

"What would be a good time for you?"

I thought for a moment. I would have to shower,
style my hair, get dressed, get Sierra ready, and have
Creole pick her up. Greg still had two weeks before he
could start getting Sierra on the weekend. "Well, it's
ten now, so how about two?"

"That sounds fine with me."

I hung up with him then I called Creole.

"What?" she answered rudely.

"Creole, I need you to pick up Sierra. I'm meeting
Lavante for lunch at two."

She let out an annoying screech. "He's going to get
that two-year dry-ass pussy!"

"Shut up. We're just going to lunch to talk and get to
know each other."

"I'll be there in thirty minutes."

"Thanks, Creole."

I swung into action. When I caught myself rushing, I
slowed down. I actually felt nervous. I almost laughed
at myself. *What do I have to be nervous about?* I
thought. He was just a man. But I really liked him, and

I wanted to impress him. And this had been the longest that I had talked to a guy since Greg.

I picked out a pink and white dress for Sierra to wear with her matching jacket.

"Where am I going, Mommy?" she asked. My daughter was such a good kid. Even though she was only three, she helped me with chores and was as sweet as pie. Although it was hard being a single parent, my daughter made it so easy and joyous for me. I had no regrets about her coming into the world. She really was the best thing that had happened to me.

But one thing I always struggled with was the guilt of it not working out with her father and me. I didn't want my daughter to come from a broken home, because I feared it would affect her and she would have the same fate later on. But then again, it would be better to raise her in a broken home than in a home with violence. I knew if I had stayed with Greg, the beating and the disrespect would have never stopped, and to continue to see me getting abused would have been hell for her growing up. She would choose a man just like her father. And that would kill me, so I knew I made the best choice I could for my baby girl and for me.

"To Creole's."

"Yea!" She clapped. She was such a cutie, with her golden brown skin, almond-shaped eyes, and a for real, for real, button nose. Her hair was super thick and long for a three-year-old.

I planted a kiss on her cheek. "Come on, let's do your hair."

True to her promise, Creole arrived on time, snatched the booster, and grabbed her goddaughter by her hand. "Don't forget to use a condom," Creole joked.

I ignored her, then closed and locked my door. I showered, threw on a dress that showed my long legs and a pair of strappy heels, and let my skinny individual braids hang down my back.

I met Lavante at the California Pizza Kitchen in Long Beach, near the marina.

After we ordered our food, I showed him a couple flicks of Sierra from my camera phone.

As he studied the flicks, he asked, "So who do you think your daughter takes after?"

"Well, let's see . . . she gets her looks from me and her stupidity from her father."

He chuckled at the comment. "She's beautiful, just like her mama. Now I know when we have kids together, they are going to be good looking."

I blushed. His comment was sweet. "Thanks, and I'm kidding. She is a really bright little girl."

I was about to put my cell phone back in my purse when I saw I had a text. I opened it up and saw it was from Creole. It read, 'Did he bend you over yet?'

I laughed.

"What?" he asked.

I erased the message and put my phone away. "Nothing. Just some crazy text I got."

"Do you want to have any more children?"

"I'd like a son."

"Why?"

"I want to raise a prince, that's why. Add another good man to the world's short list."

He laughed again. "Here we go. So you think we're all trifling niggas, huh?"

"No, not at all. I know the man of my dreams is out there somewhere. If I thought like what you just said, what hope do I have for my daughter? I've been in only one relationship in my life. It was a bad one. But I'm not bitter or anything."

"Good. Don't ever be. So if you could have a man the way you wanted, designed for you even, how would you want him?"

"A decent guy. Just someone to appreciate what I have to offer. Really, Lavante, I don't have a list of high demands. I just want someone to love me. *Man,* for that I don't think there is anything I could deny him."

His face turned serious. "I'm looking for a good woman too. Something serious."

Good, I thought. We were on the same page.

"Is there anything else you want to add to the list?"

I poured my heart out to Lavante because I felt safe telling him what I wanted. "I want a man who wants what I want, and has goals in his life. I hope I'm not asking for too much, but the most important thing is for a man to be up front about how he feels, and I'll give him the same, regardless of what it is. Just tell me."

"No. You're not asking for too much. A real woman should have her own set of standards and not accept a man's bullshit. And if he is not treating her right, she should make him kick rocks." He flashed me a smile. "You sure you don't have anything else to add, Miss Lady?" He winked.

This time I laughed. "I'll get back to you if I have anything else to add, but that's pretty much it."

"Really? No ten stacks to spend or a Gucci bag?"

"No. I'm straight. Just a decent guy."

He stared at me and said, "I'm that guy. Don't trip. You in good hands, baby."

The server walked to our table with our food. As he sat my sausage and pepperoni pizza in front of me, I spied a guy who looked exactly like Greg strolling to the front entrance of the restaurant, alone. My heart started pounding. The server then sat Lavante's fettuccine Alfredo in front of him. As the man walked inside

the restaurant, my eyes could no longer deny it was
Greg.

I blurted out, "Shit."

"Something wrong with the food?" Lavante asked
me.

I turned my face toward Lavante but continued to
look at Greg from the corner of my right eye. *I have
to get out of the restaurant before Greg sees me with
Lavante,* I thought. I feared Greg would do something
stupid and trip out. I knew that I should be able to do
what I wanted, but just in case he acted stupid, I didn't
want to scare Lavante off.

I quickly came up with an excuse. "Uh, Lavante,
what time is it?"

He looked at his watch. "Two forty-five."

Greg was now across the dining area, talking to the
hostess, with his back to me. I had to get out of there.
My eyes passed over the dining area. With luck, I could
make it to the back-door exit without him seeing me,
since our booth wasn't far from it.

"I have to get home. I forgot to give my daughter
her medicine. It's antibiotics, and if you miss a day, it
throws the medication off."

"Oh, antibiotics. It must be serious. . . ."

I stopped listening after the word *serious,* because I
saw that I had convinced him. I nodded. "Well, I gotta
go. Thanks." I gave him a quick smile.

I made a beeline to the door, keeping my head down
and briskly walking. Once I made it to the door without
Greg seeing me, my hand reached for the knob.

"Allure!"

My hearted started pounding. I thought about my
date with McCoy and how Greg had sabotaged it and
had messed stuff up between McCoy and me before I
even got a chance to get to know McCoy.

I turned around slowly and saw Lavante holding up my purse. From the corner of my eye I saw Greg's head shoot up at the mention of my name. He stopped walking behind the hostess who was taking him to a table in the same section as Lavante. I had to get out of there!

I jogged over to Lavante, snatched my purse, and slipped through the door.

Once I was outside, I ran to my car, not even back into the restaurant to see what was happening. I jumped in my car, started the ignition, and pulled my car out of the restaurant's parking lot. I prayed Greg didn't go up to Lavante and question him. That would probably push Lavante away from me for good, just as I was trying to get closer to him.

The next thing I knew, I looked in my rearview mirror and spied Greg's car in pursuit of mine. Well, at least I knew he wasn't confronting Lavante. I was pleased about that, but certainly not comfortable with him following my ass. Damn! I increased my speed, feeling my heart slam in my chest. He honked his horn wildly and pulled into the lane beside me.

I glanced at him as he made a motion for me to pull over. I shook my head, indicating no.

"Who is that?" he yelled out the driver's window.

I ignored him and kept driving, making him more furious.

"How could you bring him to our spot?" he demanded.

What the fuck is he talking about? I thought. We had been there only once before. I jumped into another lane and went faster. He followed after me. I jumped on the ramp for the freeway, hoping he would give up and leave me the hell alone. He didn't. A look in my rearview mirror showed me he was close on my heels.

He jumped alongside me again and yelled out his window, "I wish I could kill you, bitch!" He was crying.

That got my heart beating faster, and my hands, on the steering wheel, started to tremble. I hated when he threatened me or said he wanted me dead, because in the back of my mind I always felt he was going to be successful at it one day.

I went to eighty now, even though my hands were still shaking on the steering wheel. I jumped over into another lane without checking which ramp it was. His car was an older one and didn't go as fast as mine did. I glanced in my rearview mirror just as a freight truck pulled in front of Greg's car, obviously slowing him down, because he was now nowhere near my car. I signaled and got over again. *Shit.* He did, too, and he was now behind me, honking wildly and flashing his high beams at me. Then, as I sped up again, he slowed down considerably, and smoke started coming from the front of his car. Then it wasn't moving. His emergency signals flashed, and all the traffic behind him slowed. Tons of smoke was shooting from his car. But still I didn't slow down, not until I was on another freeway ramp and positive he was not behind me.

I took the next available exit and got off the freeway. By this time, I was in Culver City. I pulled over into a gas station and parked in one of the empty spaces. Once I turned my car off, I screamed, beat my steering wheel with my fists, and cried in utter frustration. I regretted ever giving Greg the time of day, because after all the bad he had done, he just wouldn't let up and let me live a normal fucking life. I should be able to date and fuck whomever I wanted to without feeling like I'd face repercussions from him. After all he had done, he should want me to be happy! He should accept that I was doing things other single women did!

Chapter 4

People at the gas station passed by my car and looked at me like I was crazy. A young couple even poked their head in my window and asked if I was okay. I waved them away with my hand, offered them a weak smile, too upset to speak, and rested my head against my steering wheel. I needed my heart rate to slow down and my pulse not to race. I waited a good ten minutes. When I felt calmer and I was confident I could drive again, I started the ignition and headed out of the gas station toward the 405 to head back to Long Beach to pick up Sierra.

When Sierra and I got home, she went to watch TV and I checked my voice mails on my cell phone. Greg had left me a total of ten messages. I didn't listen to them. I erased them all. When I went to check my answering machine, I saw he had called me at home as well.

I took a deep breath as Greg raged into the phone, "How could you do this shit to me, Allure? How you gonna bring a nigga to our spot, the place I used to take you? You know I still love you!"

I erased the message.

The next day, Sierra and I were on our way out to go to a local carnival when I heard someone knock on my door. I answered it and found a delivery guy holding a bouquet of roses, which brightened my smile.

"Allure Jones?" he asked.

"Uh-huh."

He handed me the flowers and said, "Have a nice day."

I smiled excitedly and snatched open the card, figuring that Lavante had sent them. I frowned when I saw Greg's name and *I'm sorry* scrawled across the card. Those were his two favorite words when he fucked up. His ass should be fined for even saying them. I was so sick of his bullshit. One thing after another. It made me feel like I was still in a fucked-up relationship with him. But then I knew I was the one who had lain down with him and had had Sierra, placing him in my life for a long-ass time. But the mistake I had made was not Sierra, but choosing a man like him. I paid for it for two years. When was peace going to come? *Probably once Sierra wais eighteen,* I thought. The thought of fifteen more years of Greg gave me a major headache and had my stomach in knots.

I balled up the card, threw it, and rushed back outside, hoping to catch the delivery guy before he left.

"Excuse me," I shouted.

He had started the ignition and was about to pull out, but when he saw me, he hit his brakes quickly and stuck his head out his window.

"Could you please return these to the sender?"

When Greg called me later, he had the nerve to ask why I had dissed his flowers.

I screamed so loudly in his ear that when I was done, my throat ached. "You crazy bastard!" I raged. "Stay the hell away from me!"

"I'm coming to get my daughter in two weeks."

"If you want to see Sierra, I suggest you have your mom call me when that time comes. Until then leave me the fuck alone!"

When I spoke to Lavante again, I was happy to find out that he didn't notice Greg at the restaurant, even though I know Greg walked right past him to race after me. I thought he would at least ask about Sierra and question whether I had really told the truth. He must have believed my lie about needing to give my daughter her medication, because he asked only if I had made it to her in time, and said that that night he went to hang out at Shotz. It was a bar and pool hall in Long Beach. I had never been, but I knew that Creole had been there.

I felt bad for lying to him, but sometimes you gotta do what you gotta do. If I told him I had a crazy-ass baby father, it would probably scare him off before he got the chance to get to know me and before I got to know him. And since I liked him a lot already and wanted to be in his company a whole lot more, I didn't want that to happen.

From that point on, Lavante and I spent so much time together, it seemed as though a year had passed rather than two months. He would call and tell me good morning and even phoned me in the middle of the night to tell me he was thinking of me. It definitely had an effect on my alertness at school and work, but all in all, I didn't mind. He made me feel special. So special that I didn't anticipate anything going wrong. Nothing could. The man had wined and dined me, and he was cool. So that was why I accepted his request to come over to my house one night. And I told myself that whatever went down, went down. I made sure I knocked out my homework, cooked Sierra dinner, then rushed to wash the dishes while she watched cartoons. One thing about my daughter, she wasn't a wild type of child that needed her ass whipped every five minutes. She was a well-behaved child. I gave her a bath, washed her thick hair, greased her scalp, and put her right to bed. Then I prepared myself for Lavante coming through by bathing and lotioning myself down with Victoria's Secret coconut lotion and perfume.

I didn't feel nervous when he arrived. I just gave him a hug and a kiss.

"So how are you, Miss Lady?"

"I'm fine," I murmured while looking up at him. Then slyly my eyes went to what he was packing between his legs.

Then, all of a sudden, his cell phone rang, and the song "Lovers and Friends" by Usher and Ludacris came on.

I was a little surprised to hear that from a man in his forties. But whatever. It was just a song. I watched him press a button on his phone and slip it back in his pocket.

We sat down in front of the TV.

"So how was your day?" I asked him. I scooted closer to him and felt an ache between my thighs. I wanted him to touch me. *Damn!* I desperately needed to get fucked.

He gave in to my request and kissed me softly on my lips. The ache between my legs grew more intense. He slipped off his shoes and lay back on the couch. He pulled me gently until I was lying sideways on the couch, on his chest.

I inhaled his aftershave.

When I felt his hand move to my left breast, I didn't stop him, because that felt good too. Next, his lips were on mine, and I felt his tongue.

Before I had had only pecks from him, but this was the real thing. Although I didn't like the way he kissed—his tongue was a bit heavy, leaving chunks of spit on my lips—his fingertips on my nipple felt like heaven and I didn't want him to move, so I kept on kissing him.

By this time his other hand had strayed to my thigh and dropped farther.

I let out a moan when he found my panties.

He broke the silence by saying, "Maybe we should both get naked."

It wasn't the line I wanted to hear. I wanted him to take control, pull my dress and underclothes off of me, strip down, and give me what I forgot felt like.

But he didn't. So I shyly smiled, stood, and grabbed him by his hand, walking him to my bedroom. Once we were both inside, I locked the bedroom door and pulled my dress off of me. I walked to the bed and lay on my back and watched him undress. He took his time, and I was a little anxious. After all, it had been two years since I had been with another man. I guess I should have taken notice that after he stripped down—and despite the fact that I was ass buck naked—he kept on his boxers and had a hand gripping his penile area. Maybe it was so big, he didn't want to scare me! But this was a good kind of scared, so I remained patient. He crawled on the bed toward me, with the condom in his mouth.

He leaned over me. I pulled the condom from between his lips, and he placed tiny kisses on my breast, fondled me a bit more, and then reached for the condom in my hand. He then spread my thighs apart and stood between them. One hand was still on his crotch area. It was finally going to happen. I was going to share myself with another man. I hoped it was worth it. I was excited and actually a little sad at the same time, because I had thought Greg was going to be the only man I would ever be with sexually. He was the only man I had wanted to be with sexually. But it just didn't work out that way. But still. I wanted to let Lavante know I wasn't very experienced.

"Wait!"

"What, baby? What is it?"

"I have to tell you something. I haven't had sex in two years, and I've only had one partner, my daughter's father," I blurted out all at once.

He looked down at me and smiled. "Is that all? Don't worry, baby. I'll be gentle." But he looked hella nervous. Maybe he thought I wasn't going to perform well, because I was rusty.

I closed my eyes and waited to feel him inside of me.

But all I felt was his knees bumping into me. And all I heard was the sound of him fumbling with the condom paper and him saying out of nowhere, "Damn!"

I sat up and reached for his hands to help him before my little bit of wetness dried up. "Let me help."

He must not have been expecting to feel my hands on him, 'cause when I reached for the opening in his boxers, something fell out and smacked me in my face. I screamed, horrified, and flew backward on the bed. My heart started beating. Now, I knew there was no such thing as a flying dick, but whatever it was, it was resting on my shoulder. I reached over and grabbed it and inspected it as best as I could in the dark. It was a pair of rolled-up socks.

"Lavante, why are there rolled-up socks in your boxers?" I tried to be calm when I asked, but this was some weird shit!

He turned his back on me and took a deep breath. "I'm sorry, baby. It's just that I hear all the talk about what ladies want and what they expect. I was embarrassed to tell you that I'm not packing like you thought I was. Every time women see construction workers, they think because we work with big tools, we automatically have big tools."

Well, you not packing, like I thought you were, because you been wearing a sock the whole time! I thought.

Then came the moment I regretted. What I did and did not do, what I should have done.

I took a deep breath. "It's okay. I like you, Lavante. You, not what's in your boxers. But I still hope you got *something* in them."

Dear God, he had to. I was nice, but not that nice.

He slipped back between my legs and rubbed my pussy, but I was the least bit turned on. Hell, to be honest, I wasn't turned on at all. I would have rather had a threesome with Flavor Flav and Shabba Ranks than this fool, but for some reason I answered yes when he asked me in a husky, trying-to-be-sexy-but-not-quite-nailing-it voice, "You wanna see what's in my boxers, Allure?"

"Hell no!" I wanted to scream. But I was too close and too far to turn back. This man was in my bed, and I was naked! What if I pissed him off by telling him what I wanted to really say, and that was, "Get the fuck out"?

So instead I swallowed hard and said, "Yes. I do."

"Well, it's not huge, Allure, but you will feel it. In fact I'm sure of it."

"Okay. I'm in your hands."

He lightly shoved me back onto the bed.

I tried to get a peek at it, but he turned his back on me. He was able to get his condom on a lot quicker than before, probably because he wasn't trying to hold the fake dick socks in place.

I closed my eyes just as he was about to thrust inside of me, hoping I would be able to savor the moment.

The bed creaked as his weight pushed off, and then suddenly his weight was upon me. But the moment I was waiting for never came. Something was really wrong.

Maybe he is using his finger, I thought. But I opened my eyes to find him above me, moving up and down, his head thrown back in pleasure. But I wasn't feeling a damn thing.

"You like it, baby?"

I smiled, moaned, and lied, "Yeah." It was a very unpleasing experience.

"Is this gonna be my pussy, baby?"

"Oh, yeah."

Suddenly his facial expression changed, like he was in pain—he jerked one last time into me, let out a loud moan, and collapsed on my chest.

That was it? What the hell was that?

I pushed him off of me and turned onto my side. I could not believe this shit. A muthafucking forty-year-old man couldn't control his nut? Didn't he watch that Katt Williams stand-up? He should have jacked off before he got to my house! Now he had done wasted my damn time. Not only had he pretended to be something he was not, but he couldn't even perform like a real man. It was no wonder this man was still single. I was so pissed.

"What's the matter, baby?"

In my mind, I had a lot of things I wanted to say, but my mom wouldn't exactly be proud, so I turned over and slept.

I had waited two whole years for this shit!

Maybe it wasn't all so bad, I thought in the morning, when he reached over and kissed me. Then he looked at me as if to ask permission and went between my legs with his head and tongue.

I had never been a big fan of oral sex, and was even less of a fan if you couldn't do the shit right. Although I didn't have vast experience with men to reflect on and compare, a woman's intuition told me he didn't know what the hell he was doing.

After five minutes of sucking and slobbering, and then drooling and moving his head across my pussy like he was tickling me, he loomed over me with a slick smile. "You gonna give me a little more before I go to work, baby?"

If it was like the little I received last night, the answer was, "Fuck no!" *But then again,* I thought, *maybe I can give him a chance to redeem himself. Maybe since he got his first nut out the night before, this time he will be longer.* But it turned out to be just as disappointing as the first time, and this time we did it doggy style. He couldn't even get his ass slaps synchronized with when he dipped in my pussy. I didn't like faking, but I didn't have the heart to tell him the real. That his tongue and dick game was wack. Wack!

About two minutes later he dressed and was, thankfully, leaving.

He blew me a kiss as he laced up his work boots. I pulled the covers over my chest and managed another smile.

Fully dressed and happy, he walked back over to the bed, leaned over, and kissed me on the lips. "Walk me to the door, baby," he whispered.

"Let me put on something." My nightgown was lying on the side of the bed. I slipped it on and followed him to the door.

He gave me one last kiss and left.

Chapter 5

I had just kissed Lavante good-bye on another Sunday morning. Now, see, I wanted companionship and some good dick. The companionship he gave to me, but the good dick, he just could not give it to me. But I needed to have companionship around, so I put up with the bad sex. I knew sex wasn't everything. Greg was good in bed and had pleased me in every way, but he'd treated me like shit. Lavante treated me well, but the sex was wack. So I kept him around. I wanted a man in my life, one that was respectful and hardworking. That was everything that Lavante was. Greg didn't even want to work or care financially for his child.

"So how about you meet me on Ximeno Avenue? We can get a quick bite to eat tomorrow. You think you will be able to sneak away from work?" Lavante asked me.

The thought of seeing him hard at work made my coochie flip-flop in a way Lavante couldn't make it do. But I tried to keep cool. "Yeah, but won't you be working, and don't you want to wait until later that night?"

We were supposed to meet for dinner. I wanted him to eat dinner with Sierra, but I felt it was too soon for him to meet her. Two months had passed, and I still felt I needed more time before introducing him to her. Greg had Sierra on the weekends now. So far he had been cool. There were no problems.

"Dinner ain't enough. I need to see you again sooner, baby. Just meet me on Ximeno, near the traffic circle.

We'll be outside working. There's this place close by that makes good burritos." He kissed me one last time and left.

How sweet, I thought. He wanted me to see what he did. It made me feel special.

I made sure I looked nice the day I was supposed to meet Lavante for lunch. It was May and sunny, so I wore a floral summer dress with a pair of flats. I parked on the street. Cedric, the same man who was there when I first met Lavante, was there, and we exchanged smiles when I got out of my car. There were other men around working as well. Lavante was wearing his orange coveralls, and from the looks of it, we were not going to be able to go out to eat lunch like he had requested.

When I made it over to him, he said, "So much for lunch."

"It's okay. I'm not so hungry, anyway."

"Well, you see what we do?" He gestured with his hand.

I looked around and saw two men digging a ditch, one driving a tractor, and two more pulling a long pipe off of a truck. "Yeah, looks very tiring."

"Oh, it's not so bad." He paused and flashed a glance at the other guys, who were still working. "Well, I have to get back to work."

"Well, I'll see you later."

He had already walked away.

When I made the U-turn to go back home, I saw the little Mexican restaurant he had told me about. I thought, *If we can't go eat lunch, why can't I bring it to him?* I went into the restaurant and ordered him a grande burrito, hoping that would be enough, and a large Coke with extra ice.

When I made it back over to where Lavante was working, he was driving the tractor and had his back to me. I knew he wouldn't hear me if I called his name, and more importantly, I didn't want to get in the way. A guy from his crew was near me, so I politely asked him to give the food to Lavante. He grabbed it and walked away.

Later that day, I was reading this story to Sierra. Ever since she was a baby, I had been doing this. I was on the last page when the phone rang.

"Hello?" I said.

"I thought I told you not to come back to my fucking job?" Lavante fired back.

"Excuse me?"

"You heard what the fuck I said."

"Hold up—"

"Shut up, little girl."

Before I could even respond, he continued, "Look, I'm not going to find anybody else to pay me twenty-three dollars an hour, and my job means a lot to me, so don't ever come back up there unless I tell you to. Do you understand me?"

"Why are you going off like this?" I demanded. Although I tried to sound tough, there were tears in my eyes due to the way he was talking to me. Here I thought I was doing something nice for his little dick ass when I brought him food, and he was seriously disrespecting me!

He hung up.

To make matters worse than him hanging up on me, when I called his cell back repeatedly, he kept sending my call to voice mail. I called his home number. I was shocked to discover that the home number he had

given me and had handwritten himself wasn't his. A
Mexican man answered the phone and said in a snappy
voice before hanging up, "Wrong number."

I gasped. He had never given me his real home number. Since I had always called him on his cell and was
able to get a hold of him that way, I had never bothered
to call his home number. Until now. *Why didn't he
want to give me his home number?* I thought. He had
my home and my cell number. I had given them to him
without a moment's hesitation. I saw no reason for him
not to give me his home number. I was a single woman.
Did he have a wife he was hiding or a woman he didn't
tell me about that he lived with? Or did he plain out not
want me to have his home number? Bottom line was he
had straight played me.

I called the number again to make sure I had dialed
the right number.

The same man yelled, "Wrong number!"

And on top of that he stood me up for dinner. But
there was no way I was going to sit my ass in the house.
So I picked up Sierra from Creole's house. She had
picked Sierra up from my babysitter so that I could go
out with Lavante. I called Kendra, and we met up at El
Torito for some Mexican food. It was Taco Tuesday. I'd
show him. When he decided to call, I wouldn't be there.
He wasn't the only one who could play games!

"Girl, he is tripping," Kendra said. After dipping a
chip in some salsa, she crunched on the chip with her
mouth halfway open, grossing me out. But it wasn't
just that. I really had no appetite. So I sipped on a virgin margarita and eyed Sierra as she colored.

"Which part?"

"All of it. From the tripping about you coming up to
his job . . ." She paused to crunch on another chip. "To
him giving you a fake number, to him standing you up.

Seems to me that one of you needs to reevaluate this so called relationship. And from the looks of things . . ." She shoved another chip in her mouth, crunched, and swallowed it before saying, "Allure, baby, it's you."

"What do you mean?"

"What I mean is that you don't mean anything to him. Allure, you have no commitment."

Her words were blunt, and they hurt. But I knew my friend loved me and was just keeping it one hundred. So I couldn't get mad at her.

"But the thing is, he never told me anything like that. He said he wanted the same shit I wanted."

"Come on, girl, he full of shit. What song does he have on his ringtone?"

"Lovers and Friends." I almost wished I had never told her. Now was the wrong time to tell me that I didn't look at the signs that Lavante was only after my vajayjay. I had jumped headlong into this shit, had invested feelings, thinking what my wedding colors would be and what our kids would look like, and praying that if we had a son, he didn't have a little we-we with a man that didn't feel the same way. What the fuck was wrong with me? I guess I was just so lonely and hard up from being alone that I fell for his bull. A man who had been up my birth canal and had the audacity to give me a fake home number. *Who the fuck does that? How juvenile.*

Damn.

She offered me a smile. That didn't do shit for my feelings. 'Cause this was my rude awakening that Lavante was not what he said he was. The only question was, what was I going to do about it?

"Now"—she opened up her menu—"let me see what I'm going to order."

I reached for mine. It was underneath my margarita. I lifted the drink and tried to grab the menu, but because it was hanging halfway off of the table, it fell to the floor before I could grasp it.

I leaned over to pick it up. I lifted my head and body back up and gasped when my eyes came into contact with Lavante's. And that wasn't the most shocking or awkward part about it. It was the fact that he was hugged up with another chick. I wanted to give him the benefit of the doubt and think she was maybe his kid, but he had no damn kids.

Seeing me startled him as well. So if we ever had to fucking go into retrospect, there was no way he could say that he didn't see me.

And even though he did see me and he was inches away from me, he kept on pushing past me without a word.

I sat back, with a sinking feeling in my stomach. I wanted to cry. Nothing was more hurtful than what he did. Flaunting another woman in front of me, then pretending I didn't exist. I blinked to stop the tears.

"What wrong, Mommy?"

Kendra looked up from her menu. Her eyes narrowed. "You okay, Allure?"

"Yeah." I gave Sierra a fake smile.

I knew if I told Kendra that Lavante was here with another woman and had walked by, straight dissing me, she would get crazy and curse him out. I didn't want that, so I kept it to myself.

Chapter 6

When the bastard kept on calling me, I kept on not
answering, letting the calls go to my voice mail. I was
hurt by what he did, and I also had my share of stress.
My rent had been raised by sixty bucks. It wasn't easy
paying the rent that I paid now. With Section 8, I was
paying six hundred. That was half of what I brought
home every month. This shit didn't please me too
much. After picking up Sierra after work, I stopped by
a gas station, my tank being damn near on empty. I had
only five dollars to dump in. But I had had days like
this, so if I could get through those, I sure as hell could
get through this. I couldn't stress over it, anyway. I had
a thousand-word paper to do and an exam to study
for. I wondered what Lavante was doing, but figured I
needed to keep my mind on my more important priori-
ties. But he continued to come to mind.

I grabbed the nozzle and lowered it into my tank. I
noticed someone staring at me. He was standing by a
rig and filling his tank as well. I turned away. A couple
of seconds later, as my mind calculated my list of bills
and my imminent lack of sufficient funds, I noticed
that two feet stood in front of me.

He was my size, brown skinned, with a beard that
surrounded his chin and cheeks. He had an earring in
his right ear, reminding me of a black pirate.

"Your daughter isn't too friendly to strangers, is
she?"

"Huh?" I shook my head.

"I said—"

"I'm sorry. I heard you. I just have a lot of stuff on my mind right now."

"Yeah, I can tell." He looked at the gas meter and raised a brow at me. "Is that all you're going to put in your tank?"

"Well, when it's all you have . . . Uh, what are you doing?"

He placed a credit card in the slot and stuck the gas nozzle back into my tank. "Helping a sister out."

"You don't have to."

"I want to."

The barely half-filled tank was now completely filled. I smiled and said, "Thank you."

"No problem."

I opened my car door and paused when he put his hand on my arm.

"Listen, can I talk to you for a few minutes?"

I looked around. "A couple minutes is okay," I said hesitantly.

He used that as an invitation to sit next to me in my car. The first thing he did was turn around and speak to Sierra. "Hi."

Sierra looked at him and then turned her head.

"Sierra!" I said. "That was very rude."

She ignored me.

"What's the matter?" he asked. "You don't want to be my friend?"

"No! I'm my daddy's friend!"

I put my head down, embarrassed. "I'm sorry."

His hand on mine silenced me. "No, don't apologize." He cleared his throat. "Yeah, I was stopping to fill up my rig truck over there. I own about seven of them."

"Really?"

"Yeah. I own my own business."

"You do? That's really good. What type?"

"I own seven big rigs and some property. Hey, what's your name?"

"Allure."

"I'm Derek."

"Nice to meet you."

"Can I share something with you?"

"Yeah."

"You know, I work quite a lot, and to be honest, I been hoping I could meet a nice young lady, and then I saw you. I'm a nice guy to know. I don't mind if you have a child and all. I know some brothas trip on that. Not me. I'd like to call you sometime, if that's cool."

I was silent. I knew it was as good time as ever to tell him I really wasn't trying to see anybody. My focus was on finishing up the semester at school and taking care of Sierra.

"I have a son myself and came close to having a wife. But it just didn't happen that way. You ever been in a situation where you were with someone you thought you'd be with for the rest of your life and it changes just like that?" He snapped his fingers.

"Yeah. I thought her father was it for me. I guess I was wrong."

He smiled. "I guess I thought everything would be perfect for me and my girl if I did everything for her. She didn't have to work. I gave her everything she could possibly need. A huge house, money in the bank, a car. I even got her hair and nails done every damn week, bought her flowers, and still she was not happy."

"It happens like that sometimes." I thought about my breakup with Greg. "I guess no matter how much you want something to work, if it's not meant to be, it's not meant to be. No matter how much you force the relationship, it's destined to fail."

"You seem mature for someone so young."

"I'm not that young. I'm almost twenty-three," I fired back defensively.

"I'm thirty-one, and in my book twenty-three is still young."

I stubbornly refused to agree.

It made him chuckle. "Can I see you again?"

"I don't know about—"

"Just hear me out first. I know you don't know me, and I could be anything from an ax murderer to a rapist, but if you give yourself the opportunity to get to know me, I guarantee you will learn to like, dare I presume, love me." He searched my eyes for a response and continued, "I live alone. I own a four-bedroom, three-bath house with a swimming pool, Jacuzzi, the works. I'm a very hardworking man. I also own property, Allure. All I need in my life is a strong, hardworking woman by my side. You got any dreams, sweetheart? Anything you wanna accomplish?"

"I want to graduate from college, provide a good home and family for my child. I want to be happy, be in love."

"I promise I can help you get all that."

"You have to excuse my skepticism. Men have promised me a lot, and they don't really come through. And I don't even know you to believe all the crap you talking about. Real talk."

"True, and I could be bullshitting like them. But I'm a man, and you probably ain't been with a real man yet. Any old kind of way you have a child and you can't fill your tank up shows you ain't fucked with a real man yet."

I didn't know what to say to that. But it was the truth. Greg wasn't a real man. He still didn't help me financially with Sierra. I was now on the fence about

Lavante. He wasn't keeping his word to me. And he had humiliated me at El Torito.

"Is it possible to get your number and call you sometime?" Derek asked.

I gave him my number and put his number in my cell phone, locking it in.

"Take care, young lady." Derek hopped out of the car and walked back to his rig.

After I pulled out of the gas station I turned to Sierra. "You didn't like the nice man, baby?"

More sharply than I had ever heard her, she snapped, "No!"

"Why not?"

"He not Daddy!"

"And no one will ever be . . . except Daddy. But, Sierra, your daddy and I are no longer together. And one day I hope to find another man to love me and be with me. He will be in your life as well. It does not mean you have to stop loving your father. He will always be in your life. Understand?"

"'Kay, Mommy."

I was about to head home when Sierra reminded me, "Mommy, you forgot to get my chips for the party tomorrow at La La's."

My daughter's babysitter was named Yolanda. Sierra called her La La for short. She had been going to Yolanda's since she was three weeks. I was grateful that Sierra was able to go to a babysitter who employed a teacher to teach all the kids there. Sierra had been doing schoolwork and bringing home homework ever since she had turned three. She was getting a head start. So I didn't mind contributing, even if I didn't have it.

I moaned. I had so much homework to do, and I could use that extra hour it was probably going to take me to go into the store, because I knew once I got there, I would end up buying all kinds of other crap that we needed. It always happened that way.

"All right, let's go."

I turned the radio to KJLH just in time to hear Eric Roberson and Lalah Hathaway's "Dealing." It took us about ten minutes to get to the store.

As soon as we got inside, I told Sierra, "Let's get the chips and be out."

I grabbed one of the carry carts and went down the chip aisle. Sierra had my other hand, and she was skipping. She was always so happy.

I chuckled.

She picked Doritos. I grabbed two big bags. One that was cheese and one that was ranch.

"Okay," I said.

"Wait, Mommy. Remember you told me to remind you to get cereal?"

I rolled my eyes, and we went down the cereal aisle. That was where I saw Lavante.

When he looked my way, I pretended I didn't see him. But it was too late. From the corner of my eye, I saw he was walking up to me and Sierra.

"Sierra, go pick the cereal you want."

"Okay, Mommy." She walked right past Lavante.

"Hey, baby. I been calling you, and you won't return my calls."

I tried to push past him, but he blocked me. I went around him.

"Allure." He followed after me.

"What do you want, Lavante?"

"You."

I spun around on his ass, crossed my arms underneath my chest, and gave him an evil look. "You didn't seem too interested in me at the restaurant. In fact, you pretended you didn't know me."

"I guess I was still angry about the situation with my job."

I wasn't buying that. All I had done was bring him lunch. That was it. Then I bounced. Where was the wrong there? But I let him finish.

"I'm not used to anything like that. I've been a bachelor for a long time, Allure."

"Is that why you gave me a fake home number?" I pointed out.

"It all ties into my lifestyle, baby. I don't give any women my home number. It doesn't mean I don't care for you or that I'm trying to mislead or hurt you. It is just a rule that I had long before I even met you."

He had my number, so I didn't understand why he was uncomfortable with me having his.

"Long ago I dated a young woman, and she felt more for me than I felt for her. When I broke it off, she started calling me all hours of the night. She had her uncle threaten to shoot me and shit if I didn't return her calls. So I learned never to give my number out again. It has nothing personal to do with you, baby. And like I said, it is not to hurt you. You are something special to me. But I need you to respect my bachelorhood."

"So what exactly are you saying, and where exactly in your life as a bachelor does that leave me? 'Cause I thought we had something and this was going to be more than just sex." I felt a sinking feeling in my stomach.

Then Kendra's words came back to me. *I really wasn't shit to him.*

"We do, but maybe you're confused on what it is. It's not exclusive, Allure, and if I have come across like it is, I'm sorry."

What he said hurt, but I bit on my lip so he didn't see it tremble. "You never once said you wanted anything other than what I wanted, Lavante. Never once, so to tell me this now after everything, after sharing my body with you and investing feelings . . . It's not fair." He had seriously misled me. Made it seem like he wanted to be my man, when he really didn't want to. Whereas I wanted someone who wanted to be with me just as much as I wanted to be with him, in a committed relationship. Someone to stick around, want to be there, help me fix things around the house, go to the movies with, and eventually be in Sierra's life. I didn't think that was going to be difficult to find in Lavante, being that he was older and already established.

"I didn't mean to hurt you. Let me make it up to you by doing things differently."

I pursed my lips. The harm had already been done, and it didn't sound like he wanted to offer me any type of commitment. He seemed pretty adamant about his *bachelorhood*. Still, I asked, "How are you going to do that?"

"Let me take you out again. Spend some time with you, Allure." He hugged me close.

I felt myself melting. During the time that I had ignored him, I had missed him. In the amount of time we had been seeing each other, I had developed feelings for him that wouldn't go away, and when he was not around, I had a serious void that also wouldn't go away and had me up at night. I needed a man in my life, bottom line. However I could get one. I knew I deserved more, but I didn't want to take the risk of pushing Lavante away and being by myself again. I didn't want to start seeing someone new. With what I had been through with Greg, and now with this new mess with Lavante, who knew what else I would be put through?

There was a sea of vultures out there, which I wanted no parts of. *Maybe I can get over what Lavante did and start over,* I thought. But I didn't want to start over.

That was when Sierra walked back up to us. She had four different boxes of cereal. "Mommy, I couldn't decide." One of them dropped out of her arms.

"Let me help you, sweetheart," Lavante said gently.

She stared at him with mistrusting eyes, like she had done to the guy at the gas station. A cock blocker for real. "Thank you," she whispered, her eyes still slits.

"No problem, pretty girl."

"Mommy, can I look at the candy snacks?"

"Go ahead."

She rolled her eyes at him and walked a few feet away from us.

"She acts just like you," he joked.

"I don't want to be hurt, Lavante, so if that's what's up your sleeve, then you need to step off."

He kissed me and chuckled afterward. "I'm not out to hurt you, Allure."

I let him, like a dumb ass. I didn't want to be a dumb ass, but being anything other than that wasn't going to help my heart. Despite his lack of width, length, and girth, I liked Lavante. I had invested something in him that I was having a hard time getting over.

"I'll call you later, and answer this time." He walked away.

When Sierra and I were at the register, I asked her, "Sierra, did you like the man you just met? His name is Lavante." I hadn't planned on her meeting him. But it happened.

"No."

"Why? Because he's not Daddy?"

"No. Mommy, I just don't like him."

Was God trying to tell me something through my daughter? Maybe Lavante was just bad news all around and I should seriously be done with him, instead of giving him a second change.

Lavante stood me up again. We were supposed to have a dinner at my house, but it turned out that I enjoyed dinner with Sierra, and only Sierra.

Sierra and I enjoyed the gumbo, which I had packed with shrimp, chicken, and crab, and we both enjoyed pieces of cake and milk. Well, Sierra enjoyed hers. I ate mine out of misery and snuck another piece of cake before going to bed. Lavante didn't even have the audacity to call me and cancel. That shit really hurt. I wondered where he was and who he was with. Was it the woman I saw him with at El Torito? Did he take her out and spend the evening with her? *Probably,* I thought. I wondered if he told her the same shit he told me. Did he game her, or was he being a real gentleman toward her? More questions continued to ring in my head before I fell asleep.

The next day, I took the pot of gumbo and prepared to toss it in the Dumpster, because looking at it reminded me of how I had been stood the fuck up.

When I opened my door, I saw Etta sitting on my porch, doing what else? Puffing on a cigarette. I wanted to snatch the shit out of her mouth. It was seven in the evening, and she had not finished delivering her mail.

"What's up, Etta?" I asked, slipping past her.

"Girl, slaving for these white folks. Nothing new."

I offered a chuckle. "Don't work too hard," I said sarcastically.

"Shit, I'm not."

I dumped the entire pot in the Dumpster.

***

Lavante called me, but it wasn't until eleven that next night. By that time there wasn't shit I wanted to hear him say. He might as well not even have bothered to call at that point.

"Before you start tripping, just hear me out, baby. I'm on my way to see you. And if you start that shit, questioning my whereabouts, I won't bother to come. We clear?" he told me.

"No, we weren't fucking clear!" I wanted yell. *He stood me the fuck up, and I don't have a right to question him?* I thought.

But the thought of being alone another night had me more submissive than a polygamist's wife.

So I said calmly, "Okay."

Chapter 7

He came by thirty minutes later, acting cocky like a motherfucker, like I should be happy he was gracing me with his presence.

He probably took another woman out, wined and dined her, and left me hanging, I thought again. More than anything, I wanted him to say he was sorry for standing me up. I wanted him to show me that he felt bad for hurting my feelings that night. Then I realized I shouldn't have let him smooth talk me that day at the grocery store. I should have left his ass alone. But I couldn't go back to being alone again.

"So you wanna have sex?" he asked me.

It wasn't what I wanted. I wanted him to talk to me nice, hold me, and take away all the hurt he had caused by standing me up. And most of all, an explanation would be fucking nice. But I knew at this point he cared very little about my feelings, and if I wanted him to stick around that night, I would have to sleep with him.

So I nodded and watched him undress from my bed. He folded every stitch of his clothing, including his underwear, and neatly laid it on the dresser before going to lie on the bed, on his back. I followed by getting undressed and then sat next to him on the bed.

As he started rubbing my body, thoughts of him standing me up resurfaced, and I had to talk about it, or it would bother me for a minute. So I lay on his chest so I didn't seem confrontational and said what was on my mind.

"You know, Lavante, I appreciate you coming by, but you seem to be overlooking the fact that we had plans and you just stood me up and—"

"Allure, shut the fuck up."

I sat up to look in his face. "What?"

"Listen. You have no influence in my life either way. You not mine, not my woman, and I sure as hell am not your man. So I'll do what the fuck I want," he snapped.

He was stating the obvious, but the shit still cut me. He was talking to me like I wasn't shit. Like I didn't mean anything to him. And basically I didn't. He was shrinking my self-esteem by the second. Well, what was left of it after dealing with Greg. "Why are you talking to me like that?"

"Because I can."

"No, you can't." I stood, and so did he. He proceeded to dress himself.

"I don't need this shit on my day off. You want to argue all the time. That's why your ass is alone. I could be doing better things."

I tried to look unfazed by his words, when inside I wanted to crumble. "Cool!" was all I was able to get out, because I feared my voice would tremble and I would start crying. I had learned long ago that tears meant nothing to a man. There had been so many times in the past when I had cried after Greg had put his hands on me or had talked about me so bad, the emotional pain matched the physical.

He looked me up and down like I wasn't shit. "There's too many women out here for me to be dealing with your childish ass! For every chick that's not willing, there's about five that are. Your pussy may be good, but it ain't that good. Oh, and there's a whole lot more I can say about you."

A voice rang out in my head. *Apologize. Tell him you're sorry, or you'll end up alone again tonight!* But I couldn't. I couldn't let him talk to me like that—like I didn't mean a damn thing to him and it was so easy for him to walk out on me. I watched him dress in silence.

"May I look in your mirror, make sure I'm straight?"

I ignored him and put my clothes back on.

"Fuck it, then."

He left my house without another word. I walked behind him and almost begged him to come back. Almost.

That night I felt horrible—loneliness grabbed me and I couldn't shake it. My fingers itched to call Lavante, but I fought hard and didn't do it. I would just have to get over him. The next day, after going to work and school and picking up Sierra, I cooked a meal of fried chicken, macaroni and cheese, and string beans for Sierra and myself. I read her a book before I put her to bed, and I went to bed shortly after she did.

Later that night my phone started ringing, waking me out of my sleep. I snatched it off my nightstand and answered.

"I'm at your door. Let me in."

It was Lavante. Although this might sound dumb, despite the fact that he had blatantly disrespected me and put me down, I was happy he was at my door, because it would kill the void that had been present in me since he left. To me that void took precedence over the bad things he had said about me.

I went to the door and let him in.

He strolled inside and searched for me in the dark. "Baby, why are all the lights out?"

I ignored him. "I thought you had several other women to choose from. Why are you at my fucking house?"

He ignored me and searched for the light switch in the dark. When he found it, he flicked it on. "I know you not still tripping off earlier today."

"Should I not? Look how you came at me!"

"Listen, I didn't come over here to argue."

"But—"

He kissed my lips and grabbed my right breast, shutting me up. "I don't care what you say. Come here with all that fussing." He chuckled. "These breasts are mine, and that ass is mine, so I'm not tripping."

I rolled my eyes at him, but he was too busy kissing my neck, so he didn't see. "Nothing on me is yours, remember? You're my friend. And why you rubbing on good but not that good pussy?"

To tell the truth, I was a damn fool for accepting what he offered. But despite his funky-ass attitude and arrogance, he alleviated this pang, this pang I felt when I was real with myself and faced the fact that I had no man to love me or appreciate me. Lavante was a momentary fill-in. Not because I wanted him to be, but because I could have him no other way. There was a void in my life that Oprah, self-help books, and chocolate just could not fill. This was why I accepted Lavante into my bed. He filled the void when he walked in my door, and he drained it when he left.

He grabbed my hand in his, gently helped me to my feet, and led me into the bedroom, saying, "I was just messing with you on that part, and as for the friendship thing, maybe that will change."

I grimaced inside as he kissed me all over like a pimply-faced fifteen-year-old about to lose his virginity.

"Baby, wanna try something new?" He went between my legs.

My eyes narrowed as he gnawed at my pussy. "What?"

He swatted one of my booty cheeks. "That back door."

No, he didn't! "Are you talking about anal sex?"
"Yeah. But I'll take off the condom."
"No. My ass is reserved for my future husband." *And you damn sure ain't that!* I thought. He had a lot of nerve. He didn't want to commit, but he wanted to fuck me in my ass. It wasn't going to happen.

So he sighed and slipped his pretzel stick in my pussy. I moaned like I always did to make him feel good. I even grabbed my titties for effect, and shit that was the only thing that aroused my ass any damn way. I counted in my head. I got to fifty-four, and he was lying across my chest, breathing hard like he had asthma. What shocked me even more was when he stretched out across my bed and slept. I felt like pouring a pitcher of ice water on his sorry ass. He had busted his nut and was super pleased, whereas I had felt no pleasure at all. And he was cool with that.

Again, the voice in my head, which I often tried to tune out with my punk-ass justifications for why I needed Lavante in my life, reminded me that I didn't. As the hours passed that night and he snored, my mind raced. When I added logic to it and not the weakness of my heart, I knew I deserved better than the bullshit he was subjecting me to. The only thing he was giving me was a squirmy dick that I didn't even enjoy. I wasn't getting anything else out of it, certainly not the things I, as a young woman, deserved from the man to whom I was giving myself, like romance and dates and intimacy, without it always being about sex. I also deserved a man who would listen to whatever came out of my mouth, no matter how relevant or irrelevant it was to his life, because it was coming from me.

But he was getting a whole lot out of it—a young woman with a young body and a mind. He got to drop by whenever he wanted, and he got sex out of me whenever he felt like dealing with me, with no strings attached, so he could do his dirt on the side without having to lie about it. He was winning, and I was losing. I needed to be strong and get his ass out of my house and out of my life.

I shook him awake.

"Oh, you wanna go another round, baby?"

"No. This ain't right. I'm not with this shit anymore. Get up, get dressed, and get the fuck out of my house."

"What?"

I stood and threw his clothes at him. "You heard me. Get up and get out. You got five minutes to get your ass out of my house."

He angrily jumped from the bed. "Fine. I don't need shit from you. I can go to one of my other bitches right now."

"Then go!" I tried not to yell so I wouldn't wake Sierra up. And despite how much his words were hurting me, I fought back. "I don't give a fuck what you do. Just get out of my crib with your trife ass!"

He pulled his clothes on and strutted out of my room.

"And close my door!" I shouted.

When he got to the living room, I followed after him. He opened the front door, walked out, and stood on my steps, to talk more shit, I assumed. "By the way, you are a stupid-ass broad. I was trying to be in your life and be there for your daughter."

I was taken aback by him calling me stupid and bringing up my daughter. So I fought fire with fire.

"By the way, don't call me. We're done. I don't want you, don't need you and your shit. I'm going out tomorrow, maybe to Shotz, to find me a real man, you punk bitch!"

His head jerked up as if he had been slapped. His mouth was moving, as if he was searching for a reply but couldn't find one.

And I wasn't waiting. I slammed the door in his face.

It wasn't long before he called me, but I refused to take his call.

Throughout the night he continued to call me. Finally, when he wouldn't stop calling, I snatched up the phone and yelled, "What the hell you want?"

"Don't even think of going to Shotz!" he fired back. "Or us . . . this is over."

"What *us?* We're just friends, remember? I can go wherever the fuck I want. You don't own Shotz, and you don't fucking own me."

"No one is going to want to fool with you. You'll never get more than what I'm giving you, so be grateful. You're a single woman with a child. Baggage all the way."

I didn't respond. I knew he was trying to hurt my feelings. I hung up the phone. Then I cried, because maybe, just maybe, he was telling the truth. I did come with baggage. I was a young single parent. And Lavante didn't even know how crazy my baby's father was or the problems he could potentially cause. It scared me because I didn't want to be alone for the rest of my life. I wanted a mate to love me. The thing that bothered me the most was, despite what Lavante had said and done to me, despite all the hurt and disrespect, I still didn't feel like I was completely done . . . with him. I knew I had some serious issues.

Chapter 8

I had told myself that things were over between Lavante and me. Shit, people and things changed. I felt that that was just what Lavante did, and I wanted to have no parts of him now.

After I ignored his calls for two weeks, he showed up at my doorstep with roses—twelve of them—some chocolate-covered strawberries, and a sad face. He held a poster-board sign with his home phone number on it and the message, CALL ME ANYTIME.

"I'm sorry for everything. I have a habit of being an ass. If you take me back, I'll work on that and even offer you a commitment," he said.

Sierra was with Greg for the weekend. I paused, a part of me wanting to tell him to kiss my black ass, well, after I took the strawberries. But there was something about his words. Well, they felt sincere, and what else did I have to look forward to? I had chitchatted with a couple guys in that two weeks' time, but none of them quite did it for me. I still had strong feelings for Lavante. I knew what it was. My mom had told me that when a woman shared her body with a man, her body released a chemical that emotionally attached her to him. That was the reason I struggled with letting go of Lavante.

I stepped back and let him enter my home, and bless his heart, he tried to make love to me the best he could. But I still didn't feel shit.

Yes, I had a commitment. *Wow.* But there weren't no fireworks, just more horrible sex. Although he was offering me what I had wanted those past five and a half months, the shit just didn't feel right.

He begrudgingly invited me out to lunch. He took me to Denny's. Denny's was cool, but I wanted to go somewhere special. Like the Cheesecake Factory. Or P.F. Chang's. He complained the whole time we were there, like he was getting his teeth pulled, instead of enjoying the company of his "girlfriend."

After lunch we came back home and had more bad, boring sex. I dozed off with his arms wrapped around my waist. When I felt the bed being jerked back and forth, first I thought it was Sierra, but I remembered she was with her daddy.

Then I thought maybe I was just dreaming. But when I opened my eyes, I was shocked to find a big-titty woman in my bedroom, staring down at me with this weird look in her eyes. And she was naked!

"Hi, Allure. What's happening, baby? My name Satin." She flicked on the lights in my bedroom. She had stripped down right in my bedroom, and I had been so knocked out that I hadn't noticed. I knew this because her clothes and shoes were on the floor near her feet.

I scrambled to my feet and stood on top of the bed, screaming, "What the fuck you doing in my house?" at the top of my lungs.

She looked confused. "Your dude gave me the address, said he'd leave the door unlocked. It's a surprise for you. Your man said it was okay. He said you was down for this."

"Down for what?"

"The get down." Her hands slid down her naked body. I could see she had so many stretch marks, it looked like body art. "I met him at Shotz a few weeks back."

I looked at that snoring bastard. "Lavante! Lavante!" I kicked his ass until his eyes fluttered open.

"What?"

"Why in the hell did you invite this bitch to my damn house? Where I stay with my child."

He blinked a couple times, looked at Satin, and smiled.

"What's up, Daddy?"

My mouth dropped open, and I looked from her to him.

Lavante reached for one of my feet. "Baby."

I took a step back and almost lost my balance.

"Did you invite her into my home?" I demanded.

"Allure."

"Did you?"

"Yeah, baby. It was a surprise to make our sex life more exciting."

"Lavante, the only thing that could make out sex life exciting is if you grew a bigger dick. That ain't going to happen, and believe me when I say I'm tired of you and this shit right here. I have put up with so much bullshit from you, but this is it. You threatened the safety of me and my child by giving this stranger my address and access to my house. Just to let you both know, I'd rather fuck Flavor Flav while Shabba Ranks cums in my mouth than do a threesome with you and her. Take Cotton and get the fuck up out my house."

I think he was still reeling from me calling his dick small. It had to be an ego blow for him. But, oh well. I had had enough of his shit.

"What?" he said.

"You heard me. Get the fuck out, or I'm calling the police."

"I got a warrant, Lavante. I'm gone." Satin bent her big stretch-marked ass over and slid a dress on and stuffed her feet in some flip-flops. Then she left the room and, hopefully, my house.

Lavante stood next. "Allure."

"Leave. I have never felt so disrespected in my life. Come to think of it, all you have ever done is disrespect me, from giving me a fake home number, tricking me into having this friends-with-benefits bullshit, to being verbally an asshole to me. Like I ain't got no emotions. But this here takes the cake. I live here with my child, and you would . . . Just get out." I knew after this we had to be done for good. No backsliding or trying to reconcile this bullshit.

"I'm not going to beg your ass, 'cause you not all that."

He was still going ? After all he had done to me? It was like insult to injury. I hated when you rejected a man and he tried to put you down. I wanted to say, "If I wasn't all that, why did you fuck with me in the first place?" He was a trifling-ass man that would never stop. I knew I didn't need someone like him in my life and I should have stopped fucking with him. I knew this, but I had kept being weak and taking him back, and each time the only difference in the outcome was that it was a worse hurt than the previous one. I should have taken more time to get to know him—so the real him could have come out—and not just fallen feet first into this shit. I felt so dumb at that moment.

"Get out!" I raged at the top of my lungs. "Get the fuck out!"

Chapter 9

Two months later . . .

I was so happy to have my car back out of the shop. Sierra and I had been on the bus for three weeks, while I scrambled to come up with the money to pay for the repairs on my car. It was forever breaking down. But I couldn't afford another car. With all the bills I had to pay, and without ever getting child support, there was no way.

I was super excited because I was going to pick up Sierra from Greg's house. Him keeping Sierra for the weekend was really working out well. He had been pretty much leaving me alone.

When I got to his house, I parked and hopped out of my car. Greg walked toward me hand in hand with my baby, Sierra. Even though she had been gone for only two days, I had missed her like crazy.

"Mommy!" she exclaimed.

Before I could get close to her or even ask her how her weekend had been, Greg said, "Wanna see my baby's picture?"

I rolled my eyes at Greg and opened my arms so Sierra could run into them.

"No," I said, giving my child a kiss.

He frowned at me. "Are you jealous?"

"Hell no. Anybody that can love you! God bless her soul."

"Oh, you trying to be funny." He stuck a picture of himself and a cockeyed chick in my face.

It wasn't so much the fact that he had a girl that bothered me. I didn't want Greg back. It didn't bother me that he had someone else. It was the fact that he had the nerve to shove a picture of her and himself in front of me, when I couldn't get him to take pictures of me when we were together. It was insulting.

"We getting married."

"Congrats," I managed to bite out. "But it would be nice if you would pay some child support."

"Why should I, when you left me?"

I had had this conversation with him several times. He just didn't get it. He and I had nothing to do with what he was supposed to do for his daughter. The fact that we might never get back together did not relieve him of his responsibility to provide for his child. Why should I have to carry all the weight on my own? Greg was the most selfish man that I had ever met. I didn't bother calling up child support. They weren't on my damn side as far as I was concerned. And don't let it be a woman that I spoke to. They seemed to always back up the men in their bullshit. The system allowed these men to be just what they were: sorry.

The way that Greg could just quit his job so he did not have to pay child support killed me. I didn't want to argue with him, because it wouldn't make him do shit no way. It wouldn't change anything. I just thanked God that with the little I made, I was able to provide for my daughter. True, we didn't live in the best neighborhood, my transportation wasn't the most reliable, and I often did without, but it could be a whole lot worse. Sierra and I could be homeless again, staying in hotels, like we had when I first left Greg. And I knew that after college I would get a good job and things would gradually get better. So I counted my blessings, and I ignored his ignorant-ass comments.

I placed Sierra on my back, and she giggled as I carried her to the car.

"I missed you, Mommy," she said.

"I missed you too."

I was happy to be able to take her back home.

"Can you play Beyoncé?" she asked.

I chuckled. "No problem." I put her CD in my player and turned it up full blast, laughing as Sierra sang in sync with her. She knew every single word to Beyoncé's songs.

When we made it home, I asked Sierra what she wanted me to make for dinner.

"Macaroni and cheese. Please," she said sweetly.

I laughed. "Okay. But we need to have meat, too, and veggies," I said.

"Okay."

So while she sat at the table and played with her dolls, I cooked. I asked her, "So what did you guys do?"

"I watched TV. Daddy and his girlfriend went to the movies and left me with Grandma."

What is the purpose of getting your kid if you aren't going to spend time with her? I thought. But I had always said that I would never talk about her father in front of her. So I asked instead, "How is your grandma doing?"

"Her got into a fight with her husband. She threw flour and eggs on him, and they took her to jail. Daddy had to come get me."

"It's *she*," I corrected. I wasn't surprised about what she said about her other grandma. She was fucking crazy. I saw that the dysfunction had not changed. I had put up with a lot of it while Greg and I were together—from her moving herself and her ten kids into our one-bedroom apartment to her going straight bipolar and trying to fight me. I didn't have too much contact with her, and I wanted to keep it that way. I wondered if Greg had had his girlfriend around Sierra, so I slyly asked, "Do you do things with Daddy's new girlfriend?"

Sierra frowned and stopped talking.

"You okay?" I asked.

She smiled, nodded, and started playing with her dolls again.

Thirty minutes later dinner was done, and we sat down to eat.

I noticed Sierra had been quiet ever since I mentioned Greg's girl. I didn't want to press her. So when I got ready to give her her bath, I asked her, "Sierra, why don't you like your dad's girlfriend?"

She was silent.

"I'm your mom. You can tell me. It's okay."

"No, not really, Mommy. I don't really like her."

I narrowed my eyes at her. "Why?"

"She's mean."

"What did she do, baby?"

"She told me to shut the fuck up, or she was gonna leave me at the mall."

What! I took a breath to keep my cool. Not that it mattered, but I asked, "Why did she tell you to shut up? Were you acting out?"

"No, Mommy. I asked for a hot dog."

Oh, hell no. Who did that bitch think she was, talking to a three-year-old that way? And secondly, if I had a boyfriend and he had a child, I would never take the liberty of talking to his child that way. It was not cool.

I dipped the washcloth in the warm water, wrung it out, and washed the soap off her back. Then I stood, grabbed Sierra's towel, and held it out for her to step out of the tub.

"Si Si, you a big girl. Go in your room and dry off."

"Okay, Mommy."

I stalked into the kitchen, snatched up the phone, and dialed Greg's number. But instead of hearing it ring, I discovered that my number was blocked. *What the hell?*

The next week Greg came to pick Sierra up, I confronted him.

"Why is my number blocked?"

He chuckled. "'Cause my girl thinks it's disrespectful for another woman to be calling my house, and I don't have money for a cell."

"I'm not just some other woman, Greg. I'm your child's mother. That gains me respect. And besides, I never did anything to her. She don't know me any more than I know her."

"Well, I have to respect my woman's wishes."

My eyes narrowed. "Respect? I didn't think you knew what that word meant. You never showed me any when I, the mother of your child, was with you, but you can easily give it to her. And you don't show me respect now."

"Look, man, I don't wanna hear this. I been leaving you alone, so you should be happy with that. Don't get me started again." His old fire was back in his eyes. It made me nervous, but still I was gonna say what I wanted to say.

"You know your daughter don't like her too much?"

He chuckled. "Whew! Allure, you really petty."

"She said your girl told her to shut the fuck up!"

He shook his head at me. "Why you gonna lie on a child? Sierra ain't said shit like that, 'cause Angel beautiful on the inside and out."

That comment hurt. He was putting another woman before his child. I could already see it. I could never do that. *How dare he?*

I shook my head.

"If you need to get in contact with me, you can call my mother. You know she lives down the street from me."

Oh, hell no! He really thought he was going to have my child and I would not be able to get in contact with him? And secondly, did he really think I was going to leave my child around his bitch after how she spoke to her?

"Those days of you controlling shit are over. Until you talk to her and she apologizes to my child, and until my number is unblocked, my child will not be going to your house."

"Who the fuck you think you talking to, Allure? You don't control what goes down in my fucking crib! You got me fucked up! Maybe you mad. The holidays are right around the corner, and I got somebody and you fucking alone."

True, I was a little . . . Naw. Scratch that. I was very depressed about the fact that I had no one to love or love me for the holidays. But I wasn't petty. This was about my daughter, and deep down he knew that shit. He was cold for trying to make it seem like it was something else.

So I didn't even bother arguing with him. For some reason my silence got him more turned up. When he continued to yell, I calmly pushed Sierra back into the house and closed the door directly in his face.

He knocked on the door and said, "You cold for that one. All you doing is hurting your child. She wants to go with her daddy, and you won't let her, because you jealous of my girl. You gonna regret that shit. We'll see who calls who first."

I watched him walk away from my living room window.

Truth be told, beforehand, when I was getting her dressed, Sierra told me she didn't want to go over to his house, anyway, because of that bitch he had there. So I wasn't hurting her at all. Furthermore, I wasn't going to waste my time arguing with Greg. I could show him better that I could tell him. Either his girl talked to my daughter decently, or she wasn't going over there.

Chapter 10

I smiled and tiptoed into Sierra's room. It was Christmas morning. I was so excited to see her open her gifts that I woke up before she did, although she swore that she would wake up first.

One of her feet was hanging out of the blanket. I started tickling it. I laughed when she pulled it back. "Sierra."

She groaned and turned in her sleep.

I started tickling her again. "What happened to you being awake first, huh?" I asked.

She started laughing and turning her body in different directions to get away from my fingers. When I stopped tickling her, she sat up in her bed and said, "Merry Christmas, Mommy!" She looked super happy.

"Merry Christmas, Sierra. You ready?"

I shouldn't have said that. She leaped from the bed, squealing, and ran out of her room and into the living room.

I followed after her, excited to see the look on her face when she opened her gifts. I grabbed my disposable camera off the coffee table and started snapping pictures of her as she opened her gifts. I was so relieved that I was in a position to get her gifts. Thank God. When my car broke down, I had to dip into my Christmas fund. But I was still able to get her some nice things. I had asked Greg for some money, but he told me no. Sierra screamed when she opened her Bratz doll. She was obsessed with them. She also unwrapped a beauty parlor where she could sit in front of a mirror and do her makeup and her hair, her own karaoke machine and, of course, an Easy-Bake Oven. For me it was a blessing to be able to provide her with things that put a smile on her face.

I had expected Greg to call me the night before, asking if he could see Sierra on Christmas Day, but he never did. I didn't want to be a total bitch to him, so I was planning on calling him to see if he wanted to spend a couple hours with her.

I couldn't wait to show her what Kendra and her godmother, Creole, had got for her.

"Thank you, Mommy!" she exclaimed.

"You welcome, but you know you not done yet, right?"

"I'm not?"

I pulled another gift out from under the tree. It was from Kendra. It was a pair of cute hot pink roller skates.

While she opened those and screamed, I went to the living room closet and pulled out the Barbie electric jeep. *Fucking Creole,* I thought. *She knows how to come through.*

Sierra went insane when she saw the jeep. She started running around the house, screaming. It made me crack up.

"Mommy, can I ride this now?"

I chuckled and said, "Go put on your house shoes and you can go."

She raced in her room, and within seconds, she came out with her slippers on.

I pulled the jeep outside and sat it in the grassy courtyard. There were other kids outside playing with their toys. Some were riding scooters and bikes, and some were busy showing other kids what they had gotten for Christmas.

So many girls ran up to Sierra to see her jeep. She smiled excitedly and slowly pressed the gas pedal.

"Hold on to the bars, Sierra," I advised her.

Soon she got the hang of it.

I went inside quickly to grab the cordless phone out of the kitchen. I attempted to call Greg, but I saw my number was still blocked. I sat on the porch and watched my daughter. Although this was the second year that Greg and I had been separated, it still got me depressed. The last thing that I ever wanted for Sierra was to have a broken home. Especially on Christmas. I hoped her dad at least called her before we both got dressed and went over to my mother's house for Christmas dinner. I was more than willing to stop by his house and let him spend a couple hours with Sierra. But something told me I wouldn't hear from him. Luckily, Sierra was too occupied with her toys to really care. Or at least she pretended that she didn't.

It seemed like Greg had dropped off the face of the earth. He never called on Christmas or any time after that. *What a piece of shit,* I thought. *Just to teach me a lesson, you would miss Christmas with your firstborn.*

It took Greg a good three weeks before he came begging for me to let him see Sierra again. First, he started with phone calls, asking to speak to Sierra and telling her that Angel said hi. Then he popped up without calling.

Sierra was at the kitchen table, doing an ABC's work sheet, while I worked on an essay for my literature class. The teacher was a real pain in the ass and made us do essays every damn week.

When I heard the doorbell, I went and answered the door, and he was standing there.

I took a deep breath so I stayed calm. "Greg, didn't I tell you not to pop up at my house without calling?"

"Why you got a nigga in there, around my daughter?"

"If I did, what would you do?"

"I'd put a bullet in his head, that's what."

"Okay. It's time for you to go."

But he could have bitches around my daughter and it was A-OK? He was such a fucking hypocrite.

"No, I'm just bullshitting. Let's start over please!" He looked super distressed at the thought of me closing the door in his face.

I took a deep breath and nodded, even though the threat he had made was so disrespectful and uncalled for.

"How are you doing?"

"Greg, what are you doing popping up at my house without calling?"

"My bad. I just wanted to give you the outfits Angel bought for Sierra. She said she hopes you reconsider and let me start picking her up again."

He handed them to me.

"I don't have a problem with you getting Sierra, but I should be able to call you, and secondly, no one should be talking to our daughter that way. I also feel that if you have someone living with you or staying over when my daughter is there, I have a right to know, as you would like to know. And I thought it was real pathetic that you didn't even have the decency to call and wish Sierra a Merry Christmas."

I felt like I was talking to a slow person. This stuff I was saying was common sense. But not with someone like Greg. He just didn't seem to get it, but I hoped the tough love I was showing him made him get it now. My daughter meant the world to me. I refused to let anyone mistreat her. If that meant that Greg wouldn't be in her life to protect her, then that was how it would have to be.

"Look, about Christmas. I didn't have any money to buy her anything, so I was too embarrassed to show my face over here. As far as the other stuff, I understand. Look, I already talked to Angel. She gets it now, and she is sorry. She was just having a bad day. And I should have told you she was living with me. She is. But, Allure, damn. You don't have to make shit hard on me when you see me trying to change. I don't even post up over here anymore like I used to, out of respect. I know you fucking with other men, but do you see me tripping?"

Truthfully, since I lived on the east side of Long Beach and everybody knew everybody, it wasn't hard for Greg to find out my business. And not that it was his fucking business, but I wasn't seeing anybody. But Greg had been like that since we were together. He had always sworn up and down that I was fucking everybody. He was crazy. And since he was with Angel and he was marrying her, or so he claimed, why the hell did he care what I was doing? I thought.

"See, here you go. You just don't get that my business is my business, and as long as I take care of Sierra, my personal life is separate. I don't have to explain it to you. Go home, Greg. I'll call your girl, and we can have a talk. If we can come to an understanding, then I have no problem with you taking Sierra this weekend."

As I closed the door in his face, I heard him mutter, "Damn."

I peered out the window and saw him walk away. I locked the door and walked into the kitchen. I watched him get into his car and drive away.

Sierra was still at the kitchen table. "Sierra, look at the two outfits your Dad's girlfriend got for you." If she was trying to be cool, then so was I. I didn't want any problems at all with her, because it would affect Sierra.

"I don't want to," she said sharply.

My head snapped back from surprise. She had never used that tone before. I sat down next to her. "What's wrong?"

She stopped writing and kept her head down.

"What? You can't look at me now? What is wrong?"

Suddenly Sierra started crying.

"What is it, baby? Why are you crying?" My eyes watered. I didn't know what was wrong, so I couldn't help her.

"Angel hit me."

"What!" I exclaimed, nutting up. "For what?"

"I didn't come fast enough when she called me. She used her boot."

"Sierra, why didn't you tell me? I always told you that if any man or woman touched you in an inappropriate way or hurt you, you had to let me know. Was your daddy there?"

Her voice cracked. She took a deep breath and said, "She told me if I told you, she would fuck me up again. 'Cause she didn't like me, anyway. Daddy was gone, and she told me not to tell him, either."

Tears poured from my eyes now. I felt like shit for not knowing anything about this. All this time had passed, and she had gotten away with putting her hands on my child. And Greg was leaving my child alone with her.

I grabbed my purse and told Sierra, "Come on."

I hightailed it over to Kendra's house because her house was closer to where I lived. She was sitting on her porch when I pulled up. I leaned over and unbuckled Sierra's seat belt and said, "Sierra, run to Kendra and tell her I said for her to keep you for a few minutes. I'll be back soon."

Once Sierra was safely in Kendra's arms and Kendra waved at me, I peeled out and busted a U-turn. Since Sierra was no longer in the car, I drove sixty miles per hour on the streets until I was at Greg's apartment. My plan was to whip his ass and hers. Her for doing the shit and him for allowing it to go down. I just might get my ass whipped, but still I had to prove a point. *Don't fuck with my child!* I knew there was a reason that Sierra didn't like this bitch!

Once I made it to his door, I swung my foot back all the way and kicked it. "Open up, muthafuckas!" I kicked over and over again.

Then I backed up and looked up at his bedroom window, searching for movement. I saw a chick peer from the window. I couldn't see what she looked like, but I assumed it was her.

"Come outside, bitch!" I yelled. I rushed back to their door. I banged on it and kicked it. Greg must still be gone, I assumed, because he would have been out there with quickness.

She opened the door and faced me. I remembered the picture Greg had shown me, and I knew that this was her.

She had a look that said, "Bitch, I'm not afraid of you."

And to be honest, I figured she wouldn't be. If my own child's father didn't respect me, why in the hell would she? He probably talked about me like I was a dog to this girl.

With a phone in her hand, she said, "Bitch, if I don't want you calling my house, I damn sure don't want you coming to my doorstep. Go before I call the police."

She had me fucked up. I slapped the phone out of her hand and slapped the shit out of that bitch all in one swift movement.

She screamed, and before she could retaliate, I gripped her hair and dragged her from her steps into the street.

"Somebody help me!" she yelled and tried to fight me off. But I had too much anger and adrenaline pumping through me to release her.

I shoved that bitch back sharply with an open palm. She staggered back fearfully, and I rushed her with my two fists, drilling her face with my left and following with my right.

Her punk ass tried to duck and scream, but I still got her.

"Bitch, don't you ever hit my child!" I swung again and struck her in her temple.

She swung blindly at me. I took a step to the side and punched her again in her mouth, busting her top lip. Blood splattered on the street. Soon people came outside and a crowd encircled us. I gripped her weave and smacked her in her cheek. That hit caused her to fall backward onto the pavement.

I took a deep breath, walked over to her, and spit in her face. "Bitch, I'll die for my daughter. Don't you ever in your fucking life put a finger on my child. Now, call the police, and I'll call, too, and tell them you whipped my child with a boot. Who you think they gonna be more sympathetic to you or me, bitch?"

As I walked off, I couldn't help but feel equally responsible for this shit. I should have questioned Greg about this chick the moment he told me about her. But I gave him the benefit of the doubt, thinking he would tell me if he had someone living with him or even around Sierra. I was far too lenient, and that had put my daughter in harm's way. I couldn't let anything like that ever happen again. Judging from the fact that she would put her hands on a three-year-old, she truly had to be a piece of shit. If I was able to forgive myself for that mistake, it would take a long-ass time. I didn't know if I was going to let Greg see Sierra again after this. He should have been more aware and more careful about the company he kept, especially around his daughter. And if I did let him see her again, that bitch would have to be out of his life.

Chapter 11

I was too hurt, too disappointed. Disappointed in myself. Someone had harmed my child. Something I swore would never happen. Greg had been calling my phone nonstop, but I refused to answer. It was just as much his fault as it was mine and hers. He should have known what type of woman was around his daughter.

I just looked at my sister blankly at my mother's house. For over an hour we had drilled Sierra on what went down with Angel, asking her if anyone else had harmed her. She told us no. According to Sierra, her daddy wasn't there when Angel whipped her.

Sierra didn't have her mind on it anymore after my mother asked her to help her make some candles. My mother was always making different types of crafts since she had retired from working in housekeeping at the Hyatt Regency Hotel in Long Beach.

I was pretty much quiet.

My sister had brought some fried catfish and shrimp. I had no appetite, but Sierra, my mother, and Crystal grubbed down. Sierra loved her some shrimp. I was just happy that she was in good spirits and was no longer upset about what had happened.

Afterward, my mother set up her easel, and Sierra did some water painting. She was so played out after that, she ended up falling asleep on my mother's bed.

My sister took one look at me and said, "Come on, littele sister, you need a drink."

***

We went to Market Street Bar And Grill in Ingle-
wood. Over a rum and Coke, 'cause I needed something
strong, I reflected on my fucked-up situation. The
family I wanted for my daughter, I didn't have. In fact,
my family was just as dysfunctional as the one I grew
up in before my daddy died. Scratch that. It was more
dysfunctional than my mother and father's. My father
used to beat the shit out of my mother and cheat on her
like hoes were going out of style. So she left him. A year
later he died in a bus accident. Not the traditional way.
My dad was a loser. He used to break into parked buses
and sleep in them. Someway he managed to set himself
on fire inside a bus.

My situation continued to be dysfunctional because
Greg was still in my life, wreaking havoc. The worst
thing about it was the fact that Sierra was from a broken home, and it bothered me because I had done my
best to avoid this from happening by trying to make
it work with Greg. But it was healthier to leave him. I
didn't want to say I regretted having Sierra, because
I didn't. I just wished that I had chosen a better partner than Greg. But the things he subjected me to, he'd
promised me he never would. Then I thought about Lavante. Another man I had wasted my time on, because
he didn't really want me. He just wanted pussy. He
probably messed around with me to make his old ass
feel young. And now I was alone yet again.

"I know you bothered by what you going through.
But it wasn't your fault, so you need to forgive yourself."

I instantly started crying. "I made the wrong choice
in men, Crystal, and I feel like I'm going to spend the
next fifteen years paying for it. I never wanted things
to be like this. I'm alone, a single parent struggling to

make it. I'm literally living from paycheck to paycheck. I'm lonely, horny! I could go on and on."

Crystal started laughing at the horny part.

"No. Serious. I'm a fucking mess!"

"Girl, if you don't knock it off . . . You got a beautiful, smart daughter, your own place, a job, car, and you in college. It could be worse, so shut the fuck up and count your blessings. I know Greg is a piece of shit, but you can't worry about him, because you can't change him and you can't change the fact that you had a baby by him. That's the only good things that came out of that nightmare relationship. You just focus on you and your daughter. Don't worry about him and what he don't do. One way or another, Sierra is going to have what she needs. And stop being so hard on yourself. You are a good mother."

I wiped my tears and nodded. She reached over and hugged me. I hugged her back.

I was still bothered by the fact that I was still alone. Crystal's words of wisdom couldn't do away with those feelings. Or the void. Lavante's words always floated back into my head, scaring me. He'd said I would never have a man offer me more than what he'd offered. Part of me felt that would always be true.

After three more drinks I was feeling tipsy and good.

"Girl, I broke up with Troy's ass." Troy was Crystal's boyfriend of the past two years.

"Why?" I asked.

"Oh, you thought this was just about you? That motherfucker was messing around with a chick with a hellish weave and some fucked-up-ass implants."

I busted up laughing.

"And the ho was a stripper."

"You lying!"

"If I am, may God burn a hole in my ass! We all go through stuff with these sorry-ass men."

I busted up laughing again. Everything was making me laugh because I was super tipsy. "Let me use the restroom."

"Okay. I'll be on the dance floor."

I laughed at that too.

After I made it to the restroom, I took a quick piss, came out to wash my hands, and splashed water on my face. I grabbed a paper towel and patted my face.

"Excuse me."

I opened my eyes and looked at the image in the mirror. I didn't need to turn around, 'cause I could see him perfectly. Tall as hell, stocky, too, with waves, dark brown eyes, wide-bridged nose. A younger version of Denzel. He had to be in his late twenties. I gave my face one final pat and offered a half smile. That was all I could manage.

"Yes?"

"I noticed that you were crying earlier. I wanted to come by then, but I didn't know if it would be cool. But when I saw you get up, I followed you, thinking it would be my chance. Is there anything I can do to help? Maybe buy you a drink?"

"As you can see, I'm too tipsy for any more drinks."

He laughed, and his eyes crinkled at the sides. He was cute. And all I needed tonight was to get laid. So I switched off out of the bathroom, down the stairs, and he was close on my heels.

Once downstairs I saw my sister on the dance floor. I noticed the guy was still standing near me. He was cute, and I didn't mind the attention. And all the alcohol had me a little loosey-goosey.

"I'm James."

"Allure."

"You come here a lot?" he asked me.

"Naw. I've never been here before."

"Really?" he asked. "You must not be a party girl."

"God, no!"

His eyes slid over me. He muttered, "Hell, yeah. I need a good girl in my life."

I was a good girl. But it hadn't helped me in my life. And it seemed that the two men I did give myself to had preyed on that, instead of embracing it.

Out of nowhere he asked, "Do you know how beautiful you are?"

"Please."

"No, honestly. No one ever told you that before?"

"Yes," I said. I left out, "But they were bullshitting, 'cause they were after something from me."

"How long is your hair?"

I used to be annoyed by this question. But I had been asked it so many times, I was used to it. *Brothers, a word of advice,* I thought to myself. *Because a woman wears braids or ponytails, or even weaves, for that matter, doesn't mean she's bald! Beyoncé, Tyra Banks, Ciara, Lisa Raye, and all those other broads on TV that men lusted over have all worn weaves. Yet when you see a sista wearing anything other than her real hair, you want to get disdainful. Just sayin'.*

"My hair reaches to my shoulders, but I prefer to wear braids."

"And they look good as fuck on you! I don't mind that mother earth shit. Natural."

I was far from mother earth. That was more like Afros and dreads. But I told him, "Thanks!"

"Do you know what I do for a living?"

"What do you do?"

"I'm an accountant for a Fortune Five Hundred company, and I do taxes on the side. I'm twenty-nine."

"Nice."

I wasn't divulging what I did, because I wasn't established yet. And it didn't seem like he cared. In fact, it seemed like all he wanted to do was talk about himself.

"I also live in Baldwin Hills."

I knew the area was where wealthy blacks lived.

"How old are you, and what type of work do you do?"

"I'm twenty-three, and I will be twenty-four next month. I work in the child-care center at Long Beach City College."

"Where do you live?"

"Okay. What do you want ? You didn't come over here to talk about geography and careers." Really tickled, I laughed at my own joke.

He laughed too. He had to be as tipsy as I was.

"I like you already. And I feel this connection with you, this chemistry, which I don't often find. I know you feel it, too, even if you don't want to admit it. You trying to play hard to get."

I shook my head. "I don't know about all of that." However, I did feel something, but I didn't care to admit it. I was probably never going to see this damn man again, so why not play along with it for one night?

James reached over, grabbed me by my waist, and pulled me toward him. I had no choice but to hold on to his upper arms to steady myself.

"When can I see you again?"

"For what?"

"For starters, I want to suck your pussy. Then I want fuck the shit out of you. You look like you need to be fucked right."

His words had me salivating. I did need to get fucked right.

I stared at his pants, focusing on his package. Then I casually rested my hand there, feeling for socks. All I felt was dick, and a nice-sized one at that.

"That's all dick, baby. All man, and it can be in you all night."

I didn't answer, just pulled back.

"Come on," he said. "Can I see you again?"

And you know what? I needed to get Lavante's punk ass out of my system. And relieve some stress from what had happened with Sierra.

I leaned over and kissed his sexy-ass, plump-ass lips. "You can see me now. Let's get out of here."

I didn't even take the time to tell Crystal. I merely sent her a text telling her I was bouncing for a minute.

Chapter 12

I kept on kissing those lips and didn't stop kissing them until we got to the hotel up the street from the club. All I wanted was to lose myself in him, like in this poem I read. I chanted the lines in my head as ole boy groped my ass and kept sliding his tongue in my mouth. I wanted to feel real love, but I hadn't felt real love from a man in ages, since my daddy. I remembered the time when I was four years old and I was on the toilet, taking a shit, and I was scared to get off the toilet because I saw a spider in the corner. I ended up falling asleep on the toilet. Then my daddy came and got me off, even wiped my ass for me.

That was the last time I ever felt real, genuine love from a man, the type you instantly recognized by the way they looked at you—like they adored you. I knew that love was damn sure not in this room! But I didn't care. Being a good girl hadn't got me no damn where, and it wasn't getting me nowhere tonight, either. I didn't want to be a good girl, no way. I wanted to be bad.

So I pushed him off of me and stripped out of my clothes. Then I flung my ass to the side and posed naked in front of him, as if this little experience and the pain I had under my belt made me a big girl. I wasn't no big girl. I was more like a grown-ass woman that was lost. Looking for love from a man. Thinking it was all I needed. Naw, fuck that. I knew it was all I needed. Minus the drama that came with it.

He licked his lips as I split my legs open and gave him a view of my pussy. What the fuck was I descending into by giving myself away like this? But oh well. I lay on my back, spread my legs in the air.

"You are so beautiful." That was what he said before his head dipped down into my pussy and he started licking it like a kitty cat longing for some warm milk and finally getting it. Slow, light strokes, inserting his tongue into the folds of my flesh like it was a small penis. Making me bite on my lips and causing my legs to tremble. Tossing that finger of his up into me and chasing his finger with his tongue, mumbling as I was moaning. He was mumbling, "Uh-huh, baby, your pussy is so sweet."

I knew why my pussy tasted sweet. I hadn't tasted it or anything. But on a daily basis I drank juice, mostly apple and grape, and pineapple and guava juice, too. I never had soda, coffee, or tea, or too much alcohol. I was sweet up in my heart too. But I doubted he gave a damn about that, and he probably wouldn't even get to know me. Listen to me. Damn. I was about to be burned. But he sure fucked the shit out of me.

The next day I was sitting on my porch steps, wanting nothing more than to watch my child ride her jeep in the courtyard. But James was bugging me.

I should have never given this fool my number, I thought as I listened to his bullshit. Before I'd slipped out of his car after our intense sex session at the hotel, I'd given him my cell digits. Since it was a one-night stand, I didn't think he would call. I thought he'd asked for my number just to be polite. And I gave it to him to be polite. He'd dropped me off right back at the club, where Crystal was waiting for me. I had texted her again on the way to the hotel and had told her I would be back. When I made it back to the club, she popped me on one of my arms and exclaimed, "You little slut!"

"Why are you being so cold to me?" he asked.

"Because I can."

"Don't be a smart-ass."

"I can be whatever I want to be. You ain't my damn man."

He tried to get sexy and lowered his voice, saying, "But I want to be, baby."

"So? Everybody wants something."

What in the hell was this? We had had a night of sex, and he was tripping. I was smart enough to know that only one thing could come from a one-night stand. From that point forward it would be only about sex. He had already sucked me and stuck his dick in my birth canal, so at this point he couldn't possibly want to hear about my dreams or aspirations, my likes or dislikes. I had sought only a night of pleasure, wanting to drown myself in someone. So at this point James and I had nothing further to discuss.

"Why won't you give me a chance?"

"I'm not giving you a chance for shit."

"It will be the best choice you could ever make, Allure."

"Why?"

"I just know it will."

"Whatever, James. The other night I was just lonely. And we were both after something. I needed sex and gave sex to get it, and you wanted sex, so you gave sex to get it. Fair trade."

"So you *used* me?" He sounded really offended. Then I remember he was the same man who had said boldly that he wanted eat my pussy and fuck me. And he did it all just right. Now, why was he tripping? He should be happy I wasn't calling or stalking him.

I took a deep breath and said, "We used each other."

"I don't want to use you, Allure. I want to be with you. Let me get you tonight."

"Nope." Who was he fooling? I thought. He didn't know shit about me. So how could he possibly want to be with me? Men killed me softly.

"Baby, don't make me beg."

"No, I don't want nothing else to do with you. We . . . we just fucked. That's it. A one-nighter. We were each other's jump-off." I was impressing myself with the lingo I was throwing at this man.

"You don't mean all of that."

"Why don't I?"

"Because underneath all that hardness you putting up is a loving woman. You can pretend all you want that you're not, but you are, and I'm sorry to say this, but any man can see that. The way you put it on me was different. You weren't fucking me. You were making love to me. Looking into my eyes and shit. Clenching your shit on me like you done fucked me before. And that voice! When you yelled out, it gave me goose bumps, because you sounded so sweet. And your shit was supertight, so I know you don't sleep around. I was some type of rebound. You had your heart on your sleeve. And as much as you talk all that other shit, I see through it, and you can't do anything about that. If I see it in one night, other men sure as hell see it. And you know niggas are vultures. Let me save you from the drag and the bull they gonna send you through."

My lips trembled, because what he'd said was fucking true, unfortunately.

"So what you're saying is that I'll have a lifetime of pain and heartache, huh? 'Cause men will prey on my weak-ass heart?"

"They won't appreciate the type of woman you are. They'll prey on your sweetness and your vulnerabilities. But I won't. I'd love to be with a woman like you. Sweet, innocent, without the games, and most importantly, you won't cheat. You seem too damn loyal."

He was right. All of the above. But was I gonna let him know this? Hell to the no.

"You expect me to believe that shit? That you're different from the others? Please."

"I am, baby. Let me show you."

I took a deep breath and said, "You have a nice life." Then I hung up in his face. I should have never given his ass my number!

Then I focused my attention on my child as she rode around the courtyard on her jeep. I got up and started chasing her. My thoughts were still wrapped around what he had said. I had no game, and I was a softy all the way when it came to men. I needed to harden myself up, or every man I encountered would eat me alive.

Roses were nice. They were even nicer when they arrived five days a week at my job. Each bouquet had a gift card in it, for such places as John's Incredible Pizza, Disneyland, Bath & Body Works, and Chili's. This was James's way of courting me. He had done all of this for me. I wished he'd go a little further and traded in my little bucket, which was gonna give out any day now, for a new ride. But that was pushing it a little too far. He did all these things without me even so much as spotting him.

At the start of each day he would text me, saying Good morning. He would also text me poems from poets like Jack Gilbert, Octavio Paz, and Pablo Neruda. They were super-romantic poems. He was wooing me.

And truth be told, I enjoyed it. I'd never been spoiled like that before. It made me want to reconsider seeing him. On Friday, with the last bouquet of flowers, I was shocked as hell to find concert tickets. I didn't care who they were for. I just thought it was sweet as hell that he had sent them, and I was pleasantly surprised to see that they were to a Trey Songz concert. Who didn't love Trey Songz?

So I asked Creole to do her godmother duties and watch Sierra, and I went to see him with my sister. We backed it up to all them songs, having a ball. My sister was dressed in a pair of leggings, stilettos, and a slinky top, and I wore a wraparound dress and some boots, which I tossed off as soon as the music came on and I ran to the stage.

It was at the concert that James finally made an appearance. When the concert was over, I waited for my sister outside the restroom. My cell phone started ringing. I recognized James's number. I smiled and answered. After all the trouble he had gone to, I felt I should.

"I see you," he said.

I laughed and looked around. "Yeah." But I doubted he was there. "What am I wearing, then?"

"A cute little black wraparound dress and a pair of boots. You looking sexy as hell too."

I blushed. He was there.

"What am I doing, then?"

"Standing by the restroom. Now it's your turn to chase after me."

My sister came out of the restroom and walked over to me. "That was a good-ass concert. I just want to lick Trey Songz."

I beckoned my sister to me and pressed a finger to my lips. Her eyes narrowed, but she nodded.

"Walk," James said.

"Which way?"

"Straight ahead."

I did. My sister followed behind me.

"Now turn right."

I did. And I scanned the crowd for him and saw nothing.

"Are you playing games with me?" I asked him, but I was still thinking it was cute.

"Yep."

I laughed.

"Keep going, baby. Hang a left at the corner."

I did and still didn't find his ass.

I could hear his laughter through the phone.

"Guess I'm not gonna make this any easier than you made it for me, huh, Allure?"

I huffed out an impatient breath. "Bye!" I hung up my cell phone.

"Girl, who is that fool who is playing?" Crystal asked.

"James," I said, smiling the whole while.

I followed my sister out to the parking lot, to her truck. My smile turned into a laugh because as soon as we stepped outside, I saw him leaning against a black Mercedes-Benz truck, looking fine as hell.

At that moment I ceased worrying about him hurting me, about my past, and about the risk of giving this man too much of myself. I ceased comparing him to my two past relationships. I smiled graciously and stepped into James's outstretched arms and let him hold me tight. I was willing to take a chance on him, hoping that it worked out and there would be no drama.

Chapter 13

Six months of bliss, that was what James had given me already, and it hadn't come a moment too soon. I was investing my time wisely between him and my daughter. I was still against James meeting Sierra. I wouldn't introduce them until I was sure this was going to be stable relationship. Maybe a couple more months would show me that.

Greg had come around and had broken up with that crazy heifer who I'd beaten up, and Sierra was back to going to her dad's on the weekend. James and I were inseparable. He would take me out to the movies, dinner, plays. Anywhere my heart desired. James was a brainiac, and he would help me with my homework as well. Since it was summertime—I went to school the entire year—my classes were shorter and therefore more intensive. I was spending so much time with James that when he went out of town to Louisiana for his aunt's funeral for two weeks, I felt so empty. He had invited me to go, but I had finals to do and felt funny being thousands of miles away from Sierra. Naw. I wasn't leaving my baby. Still, to be invited was really a compliment.

James had said he wanted me to meet his mother and father, who lived out there. James had moved out here for college when he was only eighteen, had fallen in love with California, and had never looked back, except for when he went to visit his family. His older brother lived out here as well, and they shared a house in Baldwin Hills together. His brother worked as a physician's assistant. He said his family was pretty wealthy. His mother was a retired therapist, and his father owned several properties all around Louisiana.

The day he came back from his trip, he called me. I was on the couch with my sister and Sierra when my phone rang.

"Phone, Mama." I gave Sierra my tongue; she giggled and gave it back.

I snatched up the phone and said, "Hello."

"Hey, baby. I'll be arriving at your house shortly."

"Who is this?"

"Who do you think this is?"

It was James. But I played it off like I didn't know, because I didn't want to sound anxious. Even though I was.

"I thought you were still in Louisiana. I just talked to you—"

"You talked to me while I was at the airport."

"Oh." I felt a little silly. "Did you bring me anything?"

"Yeah, baby."

I got all excited. "What?"

"Me."

"Oh, whatever."

"Don't you want to see me, baby?"

I dashed into the bathroom to make sure I looked okay in my tight-fitting chocolate and pink dress, and sprayed on some perfume. Sierra trailed behind me.

"No," I finally said.

He groaned, "Baby, you so mean to me. When you know damn well you miss me as much as your man misses you."

Sierra tugged on the bottom of my dress and stretched out her little neck.

I chuckled. "Oh, you want some?"

"Hell yeah," he said.

"Not you."

"Oops, sorry."

I shook my head while spraying a little perfume on Sierra's neck.

"Thank you," she said.

"You're welcome."

She ran back into the living room.

"Allure."

"Yes, nasty?"

He laughed. "Come outside, baby. I know you don't want me around Sierra, but let me at least get a hug and a kiss."

"'Kay."

Damn, that was definitely fast. I hung up the phone, gave myself one last glance in the bathroom mirror, and walked into the living room.

"Crystal."

"What?"

"Keep an eye on Sierra for me, will you?"

"Where the hell you going?"

"Nowhere. James is outside."

She narrowed her eyes at me. "Okay." A few seconds later I heard her yell, "Hot ass."

Just as I made it to the gate, I saw him get out of his car. But I pretended I didn't and opened the gate. Before I could close it, my slipper snagged on the bottom of the gate door.

"Damn." I had just bent over to unhook my slipper and pull it back on when I was grabbed from behind. I squealed.

"Miss me?" James whispered in my right ear. He kissed me on my neck, and that alone caused sensations within me.

"A little bit," I answered.

His teeth tugged at my earlobe, and his arm curled around my waist. "Just a little?"

I didn't answer, just turned around in his arms.

"Well, I missed you a whole lot."

I felt his little friend, hard and lumpy, against me. "I can see," I said.

He tried to kiss me on the lips, but I wouldn't let him. He gave me a funny look.

"Don't tease me, Allure."

From the corner of my eye I spied my sister peeking at me from my kitchen window. *Nosy ass,* I thought. Then James started kissing me. I returned the kiss, entwining my arms around his neck. My breath met his, and his met mine, and for that moment not much mattered. I was getting the stimulation—the affection— that at times I seemed to need more than food. When I pulled away for air, he grabbed my face again, tugging with his teeth on my bottom lip and laving my upper lip with his tongue. I was getting wet, so I stopped him.

"You missed me a whole lot more than you care to admit, Allure."

I said nothing for a moment, just crossed my arms, trying to fight the cold air, which had caused goose bumps to form on my arms and legs. "How was your trip?" I finally asked.

"It was for a funeral, so a little somber."

"I'm sorry, baby."

"It's cool." He traced the outline of my neck with his fingers. When he moved his hand away, it was shiny from the perfume that I had sprayed on. He pulled me closer and whispered, "You smell good, baby."

"Thank you." I held his gaze, feeling a little fearful, because I was starting to like James more than I wanted to. He was supposed to be the rebound guy, but I had caught some serious feelings for him, feelings that were a lot like those a woman experienced when she was in love.

"You know I missed you and my pussy when I was out there, right?"

I felt a jolt in my coochie at his dirty talk.

"You want to see what I got you?"

My eyes lit up. "You really did buy me something?"

"Come and see."

I jumped up and down and then pulled him by his hands to his car. He laughed and jogged to keep up with me. I sat down in the car next to him, a little eager, too eager for my own damn good, so I silently told myself to cool it. But James had spoiled me so much. I felt special. He pulled out a medium-sized box from the backseat and handed it to me. Inside were some pink thong panties and a sexy lacy pink bra.

I frowned at him. "What do you expect me to do with these?"

"Wear them for me. Show me that sexy body of yours." He kissed my lips.

I looked down at the bra and panties again. I had to admit they were pretty, but, shit, I didn't wear thongs—they were uncomfortable when you had no butt cheeks.

"Thank you," I said and reached over to hug him. I was just about to release him when I saw the lights of another car. It pulled up behind us. I couldn't make out who it was, because the beams blinded me for a second. Once the headlights were turned off, I nearly jumped out of my seat. It was Greg!

"What's the matter?" James asked.

I ignored him and sat frozen, watching Greg's next move. I guess he didn't see us in the car, because he got out and headed straight toward my apartment. I had not told James about this part of the equation:

my crazy-ass baby's father. And if Greg acted out, I wouldn't need to tell him. He would see it for himself.

"That's my baby's father. James, wait here, okay?"

"Why?"

"Because I don't want any trouble, and he likes to trip."

"Okay."

I looked at him funny, almost expecting him to shake the spot, or argue with me even, but he didn't.

I got out of the car and walked to my building. I opened the gate and walked inside to my apartment.

I stood in the doorway, livid that Greg had once again popped up at my house without permission.

My sister shot him a dirty look from the couch, then pretended she didn't see him and even ignored him when he asked, "Where Allure?"

He didn't so much as glance at the couch, where Sierra was dozing. And that should have been the only person he was concerned with. I didn't get it. Every time things were going good for me with a man, he showed up. First with Lavante at CPK, and now with James. I hoped Greg's crazy ass didn't scare James away.

"Oh, you don't hear me, Crystal?"

She continued to ignore him.

"Am I fucking invisible?"

I took a deep breath before stepping inside. "What have I told you about popping up at my house, Greg?"

He spun round. "What?"

"Damn it! You fucking heard me! I told you not to pop up at my house unannounced!"

He looked at me like I was crazy. From the corner of my eye I saw Crystal carry Sierra into the bedroom. *Thank God.*

"Oh, I guess you got balls because your sister's here, and you think you can talk shit to me."

"Get the fuck out until you learn to respect my home and my goddamn wishes."

His eyes locked with mine, and he gave me one of his "bitch, I'll kill you" looks. Acting braver than I felt, I held his glare for a good five seconds before he spoke again.

"What? You got a nigga hiding here or something?"

"You've had a woman. Why the fuck do you care?"

My sister came back into the living room and stood a few feet away from me.

"She ain't shit. She was just a fill-in until you come to your senses and let me come back. I mean, you my baby mama. What the fuck? Did you think I was letting you go?" He locked eyes with me when he said this. He was serious, and with his look he dared me to challenge what he had said. I was so sick of his shit.

I spread my arms wide and said loudly, "We are not together, nor are we getting back together!"

"Here you go with this bullshit. I came to give you some money, but since you want to be stupid, never mind. I'm not giving you shit." He shoved me out of the way and walked out the door.

Chapter 14

I followed behind him as he walked outside. It wasn't until he reached the porch that he saw James sitting in his car. I closed my eyes briefly, because I knew what was about to happen. *God,* I thought, *why didn't I tell James to leave?*

"Greg!"

He ignored me, went to the car, and bent his head into the window. I couldn't hear what was being said, so I ran over to him and shouted, "Greg, go home!"

He looked my way, then, out of nowhere, pulled a gun out of his pocket, cocked it, and pointed it directly at me. I screamed for my life and ducked behind Greg's car.

Seconds later I heard my sister scream my name from the porch steps. My heart pounded like crazy, and my whole body was shaking. I kept my eyes closed, continued to duck, and prayed to the Lord above to help me and not let Greg shoot my ass! I relied on my ears to do the seeing and the hearing for me, and any small movement or noise set my nerves on end. I was just waiting for the click of the gun and the bullet shooting right into me.

I tried to make myself invisible by curling into a ball near the back tire of Greg's car, and I tried to stop breathing and moving. But somehow I knew Greg was standing right over me with the gun. "Somebody help me," I whispered.

James's voice gave me hope. "What are you doing, man? Don't do that!"

Bravely, I opened my eyes to see Greg's eyes dart from me to James, then to the gun, then back to me again. And just as quickly as he pulled it out, Greg tucked the gun back in his pants, got in his car, and drove away.

James rushed out of the car and grabbed me. "Allure! Allure! Are you okay?"

While I was ducking behind Greg's car, I had somehow lost one of my slippers. I searched for it blindly in the dim light but couldn't find it.

Crystal ran over next. "Allure, are you okay?"

"Yeah." I looked at James. "James, go home," I said.

He looked at me as if he was going to argue, but he got in his car and said, "All right, but call me in ten minutes!"

After he pulled away, I looked around again for my slipper but still couldn't find it.

My sister watched me, shaking her head. "That stupid motherfucker!"

I rubbed the side of my face with my hand, silently.

"Come on, Allure. Let's go in the house."

I sat on the couch and made an attempt to calm my aching heart and watched my sister pace in front of me. "I can't believe this shit!" She stopped pacing. "You need to get a restraining order against his crazy ass before he really hurts you."

I nodded, but I never felt it would do any good. I thought back to when I threatened him with one before, and remembered his words. *Get one and I'll beat your ass. I'll go to jail, and I'll get out, and when I do, I'll beat your ass again, go back to jail, and guess what? I'll get out and beat your ass again.*

"He needs to be in jail, and you also need to move, Allure."

"Crystal, I can't just up and run every time Greg does something stupid."

She put her hands over her ears. "I wish I could kill his psycho ass myself, pulling a gun on you!"

I was silent.

And she said, "You know what you need to do. I know you feel this sense of loyalty to Greg and you want to keep the courts out of this, but he is a threat to your safety and Sierra's."

She was right. Of all the things to do to a person, Greg had chosen one of the worst: pulling a gun on me. What if it had gone off by accident? I could be dead and Greg could be in jail for the rest of his life and Sierra would have no parents! Despite all his talk of changing, and despite me thinking I had put my foot down and he'd got it, Greg never really had. He still thought he was in control of my life and how I lived it. He still thought he could dictate what went down and he could put a stop to my love life if he wasn't in it. And if I let this shit go, this crazy shit he did tonight, I would be allowing him to do just that. Who knew what he would try next? I was giving him too much room to continue to fuck up. I had to do something about it. One thing I knew, if I didn't know anything else, was that if anyone or anything was a threat to the foundation you had for your kids, they had to go. That meant Greg.

I filed a police report regarding Greg pulling a gun on me. Funny thing was, they told me that since the economy was so bad, they were locking people up and then letting them out in a couple days unless it was a serious crime. Crystal was so upset about this that she almost cursed out the officer who took down the report. The officer advised me to get a restraining order against Greg. Crystal loaned me the money, and the next day, I went and did just that. Now Greg wasn't allowed to be within one hundred feet of me. Nor was he permitted to call me.

I was surprised to find out that because I was low income, I could pay only a small fee, one hundred bucks, to Legal Aid in Long Beach and have an attorney help me fill out all the paperwork and help me file the restraining order. Since the fee was so small, I knew I could give my sister back most of the money she had let me borrow. I also found out that I didn't have to bring Sierra to a police station for Greg's visits. I just had to find a neutral person to supervise the visits. I had to be able to drop Sierra off with that person and contact him or her by phone. Since no one in my family and none of my friends were willing to deal with Greg, because he was so fucking ignorant, I turned to his mother. From that point forward his mama was the go-to person when it came to seeing Sierra.

I was so relieved to have it done, because I felt a lot safer with the law involved indefinitely and Sierra was still able to see her father. The visits were conducted at his mother's house. We worked it out so that I dropped Sierra off at a certain time and then Greg came to visit. He was not allowed to arrive before his visiting time, which would give me time to get Sierra there and then leave without ever seeing him. If Greg showed up earlier than the appointed time or stayed longer, it was a violation of the restraining order and he could go back to jail.

I was so grateful to my attorney that I hugged her. I think she saw that I was not trying to keep Sierra out of Greg's life, but that I as merely trying to protect Sierra and myself. Greg was also not allowed to take Sierra anywhere. My attorney said that the judge would review our case in another six months, and that if Greg followed all the guidelines, the judge would consider allowing Greg to take Sierra home with him for visits.

When I finished all my court business the day I filed the restraining order, I picked up Sierra and cooked a light dinner. Sierra and I ate, and I put her to bed. The night was so hot—it was the middle of summer—that I couldn't fall sleep. I took a shower, hoping that would cool me down, threw on a T-shirt and some shorts, and lay back in bed. I had just dozed off when I heard someone tapping on my front door.

My heart pounded a little, because part of me expected to find Greg behind that door, planning to finish what he had started, but the face behind the door belonged to James.

I opened the door, and he strode inside. I closed the door and rested my back against it, watching him.

"Why haven't you called me?" he asked.

Truth be told, I had been avoiding James because I was so embarrassed about what had transpired with Greg. Part of me also thought maybe he wouldn't want to see me again. To avoid hearing the truth, I just didn't bother to call.

"I was going to," I told him.

His eyes looked so angry. I tried to hug him, but he pushed me away and walked to the center of my living room. He just stood there, his hands in his pockets. "Are you still fucking with your baby's father?"

"What?"

"Allure, don't do that. I hate it when you do that shit. You heard what I said."

I was silent for a long moment. Finally, I said, "No. He just won't accept that we are over."

"You know, you could have at least warned me about what I was up against. All this time I've been with you and not once did you tell me you had a crazy mother-fucker who is in love with you."

"I didn't tell you at first, because I didn't think we would get past one night. Then, when I started to care about you . . . I'm sorry. I was scared it would push you away."

James nodded stubbornly. "I could have killed him, Allure."

I tried to kiss him, hoping it would make him forget that I had fucked up.

"Stop! Listen!" He shook me a little. "I could have killed him, and your child would be without a father right about now."

"What do you mean?"

"I have a piece, too, Allure."

I looked at him stupidly.

"Yeah. Under my seat. You don't think I'd drive a truck like that without some sort of protection, do you?"

"I never thought about it, because I never thought something like what happened last night would ever happen, James."

"Well, it did."

"It won't happen again. I got a restraining order against him."

I didn't want to think about it—what could have happened, what happened, nothing. I tried to silence him with my lips and by rubbing my body against his. Twice he broke the kiss and said, "I could have killed him, Allure." And after another kiss he murmured over my lips, "My life would be over."

"I know," I whispered. "And I'm so sorry. I'll make it up to you."

At those words he devoured my mouth and forced one hand down into my shorts. He pulled my panties aside and slipped two fingers deep in me. I moaned and felt my legs weaken—he held me up and continued to play inside of me. He forced my hand up against his erection. At first I pulled away, but he fingered me harder, so I rubbed him back and forth. He groaned and licked at my neck. He kept stroking me until I let out a long moan and felt myself cum all over his hand. He left me standing there, sagging against the wall, and went into the bathroom. He came back with a wash-cloth, which he dried his hands with.

"Allure, when are you going to stop playing games and let me be with you, really be with you, baby? Let me move in. Let me be around your daughter."

Wow, I thought. I wasn't expecting him to ask for that. I was flattered beyond means. But still I felt it was too soon to be shacking up with a man. And truth be told, I really didn't want to. So I told him, "I'm not ready yet."

"Not ready? What do you mean? It's been over six months. What more do I need to do to show you that I want to be with you?"

"What if it doesn't work out? What the hell will I have left?"

"Left of what?"

"Myself. I have been through enough. I can't get hurt again," I said firmly.

"Why would you think I'd do you like that?"

"Because I've been done that way before and it hurts, and I don't want anything like that to happen to me again!"

"Oh God, Allure. I would never do anything to hurt you, baby."

"How am I supposed to believe that, James?"

"Because I'm telling you."

"Men have told me that before. I've had my heart broken before. James, I can't just go by words."

"Then what can you go by?"

"Actions."

"Baby, haven't I showed you that I'm not going nowhere? Your baby's father could have fucked up my world last night, and I'm still here. If that doesn't show you that I want to be right by you, then I don't know what will!"

"What if I were to fall in love with you and you decided to start tripping, dipping out? You know how you men do."

"Is that what this is about?"

"Some of it is. The rest is about me. I'm trying to share my life with somebody. I'm not some teenybopper running around. I have a child, so what applies to those types of women just can't apply to me because of that. I have to be constantly aware of what I do and who I bring home to her. And chances are that's going to be one man . . . for life. I'm not trying to run around with several of them. I need to give my daughter a stable life. What I am saying is that you have to be real with me. Right. Or you need to walk out that door."

"I will be, baby."

"How do I know that, James?"

"It's called trust, Allure. Baby, you have to trust me, or we're not going to get anywhere."

"I do trust you, but—"

"But what?"

"I'm just scared."

"Scared of what?"

"Getting my heart broken again. I don't think I'll be able to deal with it again." I started to cry weakly. I didn't want to, but I couldn't help it.

He sighed deeply. "Allure, come here."

I walked over to him.

"Look at me, baby."

I did.

"I'm not going to do anything to hurt you. I'm not going anywhere. Allure, I love you. Understand?"

I gave him a big ole Kool-Aid smile upon hearing that. And he sounded sincere. So I let him hold me.

Chapter 15

"When are you going to say it, baby?"

"Say what?" I asked James.

Finally, I had let him meet Sierra, and we were in San Diego, at Sea World. James had got us a room out there. Sierra was snoring in the bed across from us, while James cuddled with me in the other bed. It felt good, oh, so good, to finally have a man that cared about me.

Three months had passed since the whole gun situation, and I was back in school, I had graduated from Long Beach City College and was starting my first semester at Cal State, Dominguez Hills. I was able to get a job in their child development center as well. James was so proud of me. He had kept his word and had been treating me like a princess. Now it was nine months and counting that we had been together! Sierra had grown to care for James. I hoped he didn't disappoint her.

"Look, it's something you gotta give me time on," I added.

He chuckled. "You know damn well you love me, girl. But I'll give you all the time you need." He reached over me and turned out the lamp. Then he held one arm in the air so I could lay my head on his chest. Man, I loved doing that! There was just something about waking up in a man's arms. It made me feel safe, protected. Like I could be soft, vulnerable. As a single parent, it seemed like I always had to be strong, rigid.

When I felt my eyes get heavy and my body relaxing, I whispered, "James."

"Yes, baby?"

"I do love you." Then I drifted off to sleep.

Soon I was dreaming. Must have been wet dream. Naw, women don't have wet dreams. Still, I was dreaming that James was fucking my brains out with his dick and I was wet.

"Ooh, yeah, baby," I moaned when he slid his dick out, then shoved it in only a little. "Don't tease me, baby."

He shoved it in a little more, raised my legs to his shoulders, and ran his tongue across my nipples.

I moaned again. "Oooh, baby." I felt the muscles in my pussy tighten up. I felt him go harder and deeper, to the hilt. I felt my head hit the headboard of the bed. That was when I knew . . . I wasn't dreaming. James was making love to me while I was asleep.

My eyes shot open. I blinked them a couple times, until they focused. James was over me, having a good old time.

He licked my nipples again and sensations hit me, but still I asked, "James, couldn't you have woken me first?"

He looked at me and kissed my tart mouth with his tart mouth. "I did wake you up."

"You got a condom on, don't you?" I asked.

"Yes, baby. Let Daddy get his."

He was using his fingers to massage my clit while he pumped into me.

I moaned and stroked his head, which was on my chest, and he played with my nipples again with his tongue.

He kept on rubbing my clit and entering me until I felt my legs begin to shake, and then he went deeper and deeper until we both exploded at the same time. Then I fell right back to sleep.

Something isn't quite right with me, I thought as I ran out of my syntax class for the second time today to throw up. First, I assumed it was the tacos I had last night, but if that was the case, Sierra would be throwing up, too, and her babysitter would be blowing up my cell phone. Then I thought maybe, just maybe, I had caught a stomach flu. But stomach flu didn't make you sleepy, and I had no diarrhea and fever. I just kept puking up everything I shoved down my throat! Finally, it dawned on me that I might be pregnant.

The doctor confirmed it for me. I was pregnant. But how in the hell could I be? Especially after the shit Greg had done to me, giving me chlamydia. In addition, I had always been adamant about condoms. So how in the hell could I be pregnant? I was eight weeks along according to the doctor. See, my period was irregular, so sometimes two or three months went by and I wouldn't have a period. Most said I was lucky to be this way. And I was, but it just sucked in situations like this.

"How many?" I asked. I had to make sure he'd said what he said.

"You are eight and a half weeks along."

I counted back and muttered, "Oh God." So the San Diego trip was when I got knocked up. Seemed impossible, because I had bought a big box of Magnums when we were there.

While Sierra jumped with joy at the news, I sighed. The last thing I needed was a baby right now. I was only twenty-three and was still in college. *What the hell?* I instantly felt disappointed with myself. I felt I was careful, even though nothing was 100 percent. Financially, I could not afford another child. Dread filled me. All another baby would do right now was slow me the fuck down. But I also knew there was no way I was getting an abortion, so I had no choice but to get ready for another baby. And hopefully, since James had a job and we were together, he could give me some support. I didn't quite know how he would take it, if it would make him happy or not. But no matter his response, I had to tell him. Therefore, I wasted no time calling James's ass.

As soon as he picked up at work, I shouted into the phone, "I'm pregnant!"

Silence.

I gave him a few seconds before repeating, "I'm pregnant."

"Yeah, I heard you. How did this happen, Allure?"

"To tell the truth, I don't know, James, because we always use condoms."

He took a deep breath. "Baby, let me call you back in an hour."

"Okay, I'm—"

Before I could finish, he hung up the phone in my face.

Now that hour was more like two, then three, then four. Then a day passed. Then more days came and went, turning into a week, and he still hadn't called me. And that would have been fine and all if he were dead or incarcerated or if my ass wasn't now nine weeks pregnant. It bugged the shit out of me. So that was why when I woke up that Saturday, I stomped into the kitchen to call his number. Before I could, however, my phone rang.

My heartbeat sped up out of excitement, then partly out of relief, 'cause I knew it had to be James.

"Hello."

"Allure."

My heart sank. It wasn't James, but a female. I recognized the voice instantly. It was Greg's crazy-ass mother, San.

"Yes?" I asked impatiently.

"Baby girl, I need you to get over to my house now, girl, now!"

Since it was Saturday and Sierra was over there, instantly I panicked.

My heartbeat sped up again, and I grabbed my keys and rushed out to my car, sobbing as I went, praying that Sierra was okay!

I did fifty on the streets, praying a cop wouldn't stop me. I squeezed into a spot on the street in front of San's house, got out of my car, and walked as fast as I could to the front door.

San was on the porch, pacing.

"Where's my baby?" I demanded.

"Sierra is okay. She's in the kitchen, eating some Top Ramen. It's not her I'm worried about. It's Greg."

If I had known this was about her punk-ass son, I never would have come. "It's not *him* I'm worried about," I muttered. "Why did you have me come over here? I'm not with him, so I don't care about what he's going through." I turned to leave.

She grabbed my arm and held it, stopping me from leaving. "Listen! Sierra told him that you were pregnant, so Greg went crazy and threatened to kill himself. He got some of my prescription pills and is trying to take 'em."

"What?" My eyes widened. "You got my baby around this shit?" I walked past her to the kitchen and saw my daughter sitting at the table, gobbling down some noodles.

"Mommy!" she exclaimed.

"Come on," I told her.

Greg's mama yanked me back into the living room. "Sierra, stay put!" she yelled as she pulled me. "Do you want her father to die?" she whispered. "'Cause that's what's going to happen."

"I'm not a doctor. Why didn't you call the police?"

"I didn't call the police, because I didn't want them to whip his ass. You know the Long Beach police hate him. Hell, they'd probably encourage him to do it. Plus, I don't want the courts to find out, or they won't let him see his daughter again."

"I'm not a therapist, either, San. I'm just his baby mother."

"And he still loves you like you two were still together. Please talk some sense into him before I lose my son." Her hands started shaking, and she started sobbing.

I glared at her for a few seconds before I huffed out an impatient breath. "Where is he?"

"In my bedroom."

"Take my baby outside before I do anything," I ordered.

"I'll take her to get some ice cream down at the Rite Aid."

I nodded and walked to the bedroom. The door was closed, so I knocked.

"Greg?"

He didn't respond.

I put my ear to the door and could hear somebody sobbing and music playing. I reached for the knob and turned it. I opened the door slowly and entered the room. I tried to remain patient. The music was coming from an iPod. I almost nutted up at that. I knew his broke-ass mama didn't own an iPod. She was on general relief, and that was how she got by, she and her husband. So I knew it had to be his. He was playing "Like You'll Never See Me Again" by Alicia Keys. It was our song when we were together. Across the bed were pictures of him and me, pictures of me alone, and pictures of Sierra, him, and me. Every picture had me in it. He was stretched across the bed with a bottle of pills in one hand and a shredded-up picture of me in the other.

"What are you doing, Greg?"

His eyes shot my way.

He looked me up and down and started sobbing. It was as if looking at me, seeing me, gave him the confirmation he needed, I guess. My cheeks were puffy, the same way they'd been when I was pregnant with Sierra.

"You pregnant, Allure?"

I twisted my lips to one side. "Greg . . ."

"Are you?" He stood suddenly, making me jump. "I'm not gonna hurt you, Allure." He stood in my face. "Just tell me. Are you?"

"Greg?"

"Are you!"

"Yes."

His eyes teared up again, and a cluster of tears ran down his face.

Before I could stop him, he pulled my blouse up so my belly was exposed. I wasn't that big, but a pouch was visible and my breasts were swollen to the point that they had already gone up a size. The same signs as before. He saw all of this, and more tears ran down his face.

He released my shirt and took a step back. "So I guess it really is over for you and me."

Now, see, this was as good a time as any to throw in his face all that shit he had talked about Angel, and all the times I'd warned him in the past that if he didn't stop beating on me, I would leave him and he would regret the day that I did. He had always said he would find someone better than me. I could have thrown all of that in his face. Laughed at his tears for every time he dismissed or laughed at mine. I remembered all the times I begged him just to be decent, to be humane to me, and he wouldn't. Now I had great chance to play dirty. Get my vengeance. But I didn't. Why the fuck couldn't I play dirty? Do people like they had done me? I had to get out of that shit, being the nice girl. But I guess I couldn't, because I guess that was who I really was.

"Greg, it was over between me and you a long time ago. This baby didn't have anything to do with it."

He sobbed.

"You're just gonna have to deal with it."

When he spun around, there was fire in his eyes. He rushed toward me. I instantly felt fear that he would beat my baby out of me. But I didn't let him see my fear, because I knew he would feed off of it. So I kept my face calm, despite the fact that inside I was terrified that he would hurt my baby and me.

My look must have been convincing, because it stopped him.

"Do it. Hit me. Beat me. Kill me," I told him. "It ain't ever going to make me do something I can't do . . . and that's love you again. You had everything I had to offer, and you ruined it for yourself. I'm not going to sit up here and pacify you. It is over. You need to move on with your life. And if there was any indicator that you not someone I should be with, all the shit you done these past two years is."

"I love you, Allure."

I pulled my lips in. "Then I'm sorry to hear that, Greg. 'Cause it doesn't make a difference. Because I will never, ever love you or want to be with you again. It's not healthy, and it's not safe for Sierra or me. "

He nodded.

"If you want to be in Sierra's life, then that's fine, but I don't need any more of this craziness from you. Move on, Greg." I held my hand out for the bottle of pills in his hand.

He hesitated, then shoved it in my hand. It was a bottle of Vicodin.

Truth be told, I felt bad for Greg. The fact that he had tried to kill himself was horrible. It seemed like it was such a struggle for him to accept the fact that we were done. If he had just treated me right, I would have stayed with him, because that all I had ever wanted. At one point in my life I had truly and deeply respected and loved Greg. I had made him my everything and had gone out of my way to make him happy. And he had made my days hell on earth.

He had broken me down so bad, to the point that I had started to feel not only that I deserved his abuse but also that it was my fault and no other man would love me besides him. He had almost destroyed me. Funny thing was, I didn't think it would take him this long to get over me and move on. I felt just as bad as he did that our family unit had to split up. But at the end of the day it was what was best. It should serve as a lesson to him to keep his hands and his dick to himself, get counseling, and not hurt who he loved. The last thing I wanted was for Sierra to grow up and sit around, letting a man beat her ass. Then the cycle would continue, and I didn't want that.

I turned on my heel and walked toward the door. He was still sobbing behind me.

"Allure."

I stopped, turned around, and faced him. I tried to keep a calm look on my face so he stayed calm with me.

"I will always love you, Allure. No matter what, I know I'll never meet another woman like you. Somehow they will never measure up to a certain standard, because I'm going to always compare them to you. That's why Angel hated Sierra so much, because she came from you. The worst thing I could have ever done was to lose someone like you." His sobs caused him to start choking on his words. "And the worst thing about it is that no matter how much I say I'm sorry or try to make it right or strive to be a better man, you won't accept me back."

What could I say to that? So I said nothing. I had said all that I could say to him. I couldn't change what he felt in his heart any more than he could change what was in mine. I walked through the door and kept walking. I appreciated what he had said. It was nice that he thought of me as a good woman. But he had to move on, because we were done and the way he felt now about me couldn't undo all the bad he had done. It just couldn't. I didn't want to hate Greg at all. I wanted to be able to get along with him so we could raise Sierra without the fighting, arguing, violence, and shit. Those were the things that I had experienced when we were together, and those were the things that had caused me to leave him.

Greg couldn't carry on like this forever. He had to move on, and I hoped this baby was the incentive to do so. I knew no matter his circumstances, if he won the lotto, or if he became a completely different person, I could not go back to him. I couldn't love him again. He had traumatized and scarred me. Even if he never, ever hit me again, the fact that he had done it would always live with me. At the same time I didn't want to hate him forever for it, because that would make me bitter. But I knew I deserved to be with a man who would cherish me and who knew how to control his anger and rage.

Chapter 16

When I went home, I knew I had other business to attend to: James's punk ass. My guess was that he was screening his calls, because he refused to answer when I called, and prior to me telling him that I was preggers, he always answered or called me right back. For the past week he had done none of this.

So I went over to Kendra's house and called his trifling ass.

"Are you avoiding me or something?" I asked him after he answered. I must have caught him off guard, because he had a hard intake of breath.

"No, Allure, I've been busy." At least he recognized my voice.

"But you usually call me every day. Even on your busiest days you've managed to squeeze a call to me in."

"Well, I couldn't this week," he sort of snapped. Then I heard him mumble, "I should have never—"

"You should have never what?"

"Nothing."

"What's wrong with you?"

"Look, I'm under a lot of pressure right now and—"

My heart started pounding. I took a deep breath and prepared myself for my next question. "Are we done?"

"I've done a lot of thinking about us, and I realized with my life, my career that—"

"Spare me the bullshit, and just say it, James!" Tears shot out of my eyes; I brushed them away with the back of my hand.

"I can't be in a relationship with you. I can't give you that."

"How odd that all these months that's all that you wanted, but all of a sudden, after you find out I'm pregnant, you don't want it anymore?"

"It's not about that. My life is far too busy for a family."

"What kind of fucking man are you, James?"

"Look, I have to get back to work." He didn't wait for me to reply. He just hung up the phone.

I started crying tears of anger, hurt, and frustration. I was pregnant, and the man who had said he would never hurt me just did. I was now alone, with one kid and another baby on the way. This scared the shit out of me and made me never want to love another fucking man again. But at the end of the day I knew that in a good seven months I would be bringing a life into the world, and I had to get ready for it. But for the time being I just could not stop crying.

The thing I hated the most about being pregnant was those damn doctors' appointments. Having the doctor shove his big-ass fingers up in me like he knew me like that. And you couldn't let him see the least bit of discomfort on your face. He'd make some type of shitty comment, like, "Don't you have sex?" Yeah, but I guess what I hated even more than that was going to that doctor alone. No man, no husband. Nothing. What was far worse was that it seemed that I would be raising this baby solo. James had stuck to his word and never called me again.

***

After my doctor's appointment, I took Sierra to the park. I was surprised to see an old face there, Derek. The dude I had met the year before. I was pushing Sierra on the swings when he came toward us with a cute little boy. I usually took her to MacArthur Park, because it was close to where we lived. We had never come to this particular park before, but on the way home from my doctor, Sierra had spied it and had begged me to let her play there. It was a lot nicer than the park by our house. It had ducks to feed, and it was a whole lot cleaner.

As Derek approached us, I waved at him. His son ran past him and rushed to an available swing.

"How you been?" he asked, standing beside me and pushing his son on the swing.

"Good."

He narrowed his eyes at me like he didn't believe me. I knew I probably looked down, because that was how I felt about my situation. And it was a little awkward seeing him because, after all, I had taken this man's number and had never called him. Now he was up in my face. So I tried to play it off.

"It's been a while, huh?" I asked.

"Yeah. I waited for your call and never got it."

"Sorry. I was going through a lot of stuff at that time."

He smiled at his son, who was giggling, as he pushed him on the swing. "Well, the number is still the same."

"Okay." But the last thing on my mind was calling another man, so I changed the subject. "How often do you come to this park?" I asked him.

"Once a week."

Hmmm. I wondered if he'd noticed the small hump in my tummy, a clear indication that I was pregnant. Then I figured he hadn't, partly 'cause I was wearing sweats and partly 'cause his eyes didn't drop past my eyes.

"So what's your son's name?"

"Xavier."

I smiled at the adorable little boy. "He's a cutie," I said.

"Thanks."

"Mommy," Sierra yelled.

"Yes, baby?"

"I'm hungry."

I turned back to Derek. "Well, I guess I'll get going." I offered him an awkward smile. "Hope to see you again."

His eyes locked with mine, like he didn't want to see me go. "Take care, Allure."

Derek became my new park buddy. Like clockwork I just so happened to show up at that park, and like clockwork so did he and his son. I knew it wasn't just on his end. I was lonely and needed companionship, a man to talk to. It got to the point where he knew everything about me except my current relationship situation, but I knew it was just a matter of time before he questioned me on it.

"Can I ask you a question?"

I nodded. "Go ahead."

"Are you single?"

I took a deep breath. "My situation is kinda complicated, Derek. It's even complicated to explain."

We were both sitting on a bench, while Sierra and his son played in the sandbox. They looked so cute together.

He reached over and grabbed my hand in his. "Try me, Allure."

I pulled away, slid my hands down my tummy. "Well, for starters, I'm pregnant. But I'm sure you guessed that by my belly, right?"

He nodded.

"But I'm pregnant without—"

Before I could finish, a pair of Stacy Adams stood in front of me.

"Allure."

My eyes slid up and spied an angry-looking James. *What the hell?*

He turned and looked pointedly at Derek, then looked back at me.

I gave him a blank look.

Chapter 17

James huffed out a breath, like I was trying his patience by continuing to sit next to Derek.

"How you doing, man?" he asked Derek sharply.

"Fine. And you?"

James didn't reply. He clenched his jaw. He turned to me. "Baby, can we talk?"

Baby?

I stood to my feet. "Derek, could you keep an eye on Sierra while I go over there. It won't take but a *minute*." I looked pointedly at James when I said *minute*, letting him know he better make this shit fast. But he was too busy stabbing Derek with his eyes.

Derek said, "No problem," and kept his eyes on the kids, biting his bottom lip. His arms were crossed over his chest.

But James said, "Naw. *I'll* keep an eye on Sierra." He challenged Derek with his eyes. "We just going over there."

I walked slowly away to the edge of the playground, not too far from Sierra. James followed. Then I leaned back against the gate. James stood in front of me.

"What?"

'Whatchu mean, what?" he demanded angrily.

"What do you want, James?"

"Who is that nigga?"

"None of your damn business."

"Allure, it is my business."

"How you figure that? You broke up with me, re-member? How the hell did you find me, anyway?" I stormed.

"I followed you a couple times to your appointments. That's how I found out about your little park dates."

"Oh, so you stalking me like Greg? Do I need to get a restraining order against you too?"

"No, baby. The last thing I would ever do is hurt you like that sick bastard. Now, are you gonna tell me who he is?"

"No. What I do now is not your business, like I said. Let it resonate through your head."

He shook his head at me, and his cheeks were poked out in frustration. He had no answer. After a moment, he said, "You fucking that nigga?"

"Okay, this conversation is over, goddamn it." I walked off, yelling as I did, "You bastard, you left me pregnant, and now you wanna question what the hell I do? You got me fucked up, James."

I went and sat back down next to Derek and pre-tended James wasn't still standing in the spot where I'd left him. I ignored him even when he jumped in his truck and skidded down the street.

Fuck you, James.

A few days later, like a dumb ass, I allowed my anger to melt when I arrived home after picking up Sierra after work.

James was sitting on my porch with a bouquet of flowers.

"There she is!" Etta was standing near the mailboxes, with a big-ass smile plastered across her face.

When he saw me, he smiled confidently.

Instead of walking over to him, I made a U-turn and headed back toward my car with Sierra in tow.

"Mommy, that's James!" Sierra said.

"I didn't see him," I lied.

"Allure!" He chased after me.

I was gonna keep on walking, but he grabbed my arm and spun me about to face him.

"Baby, don't do me like this. Listen to me."

I avoided his eyes so he didn't see the tears that had formed in the corners of them. Because of what he did.

"Listen, baby, I was a fucking asshole to you, plain and simple."

I continued to grasp Sierra's hand and blinked rapidly to prevent my tears from falling.

"I'm sorry for hurting you, and I wanna be there for you, Sierra, and my baby. If you'll let me."

"What are you talking about, James?"

"I wanna be with you. And I'll be right. I'll be so good to you. Help you out, cook, play with Sierra when you too tired to play with Sierra, clean up so you can study, take her to school so you can sleep late. Rub cocoa butter on your belly so you don't get stretch marks. Come on, baby, stop crying."

He started rubbing the tears off of my face.

And I let him. I grew weak and didn't stop him.

"What you did hurt, James. It hurt!" I took a deep breath.

"I'm gonna fix this shit. I'm so sorry. Just give me another chance."

I was scared as hell to put my heart on the line for James again. He had lied: he had promised me he wouldn't hurt me and he had. Of all the times to leave a woman, he had left me while I was pregnant.

"Come on, baby. What do you say?"

I didn't want to go through my pregnancy alone. I also wanted a man by my side to help me raise this baby. So I told him, "If I do this, you have to be serious. That stuff you did, don't do it again."

"I won't." He kissed me long and smooth before scooping Sierra up in his arms.

"You and Sierra can move in with my brother and I, Allure. The place is bigger, and we can do a nursery there."

I pulled away from James, who was cuddling with me in my bed as we tried to figure out what was best in terms of our living situation. The day before, we had found out the sex of our baby. A boy. James was ecstatic about that. He had started talking about putting him in football and basketball. As for me, it didn't matter, and yet it did. I had no real gender preference, but I feared that if something happened and I had to raise my son alone, he would fall victim to gangs and would end up in prison. I just felt that a father always needed to be there for his children, especially his sons. And with black women that wasn't always the case.

"So what do you think, baby?"

I just wasn't comfortable giving up my Section 8 and moving in with James and his brother. For me, it was a dumb move, because there was always the chance that James could start tripping again or that it wouldn't work out. "Look, I'm cool where I'm at, James, because it is mine. I'm not going to move in with you, and you have a change of heart and kick me and my babies out. Now, if we were married and we bought a house with both our names on it, then that's different."

He nodded. "Well, I already own a house, baby. With my brother." He took a deep breath. "I see I'm gonna have to do a lot of proving that I'm here to stay 'cause of all the bullshit I already did, huh?"

I didn't answer. I just kept my hands on my tummy to feel the baby kick. I was now five months pregnant.

For a while James helped out the way a soon-to-be father was supposed to. He would get me the foods I craved, take me to school and work, pick me up, take Sierra to the babysitter, and scoop her up and take her to the park when I was too tired to play with her. He even enrolled her in ballet class. And I knew she loved him for it. At night, when he got off work, he would come home and rub cocoa butter on my tummy, then spoon with me. He was doing everything he had promised he would do. But you know damn well peace don't last for too long.

My seventh month of pregnancy was when I saw the difference. First, there were little things. He became less doting. He stopped with the cocoa butter on my tummy and didn't care too much at all about spooning with me. One afternoon he snapped at me when I asked him if he was going to take Sierra to ballet practice.

"Why you gotta be so lazy?" he asked me. "Take Sierra yourself."

With me being a sensitive wreck because of my hormones, comments like those just set me off, and I would go into my bedroom and cry. The first couple times this happened, he would come in the room and comfort me, saying, "Baby, I'm sorry. I'm just stressed with work." Then he offered me no comfort at all. Things digressed from there to where he started saying he had to work late. Then, while he was working late, he made no effort to answer his cell when I called him. When I confronted him, he would say, "I'm working. I can't get shit done with you blowing up my phone, so I turned it off. Why are you questioning me, anyway?"

Next, our sex life changed. James had always told me that virgin pussy and pregnancy pussy were the best. He said I was so moist. And every time I turned around, he was rubbing on me, licking and sticking me. My now plump booty and even bigger breasts drove him insane. Now I could be ass buck naked in the bed, and it wouldn't faze him.

This all continued into my eighth month. *Damn,* I thought sadly as I sat on the couch, reflecting on my situation. We just couldn't make it through. And it made me hella sad. Because I felt like it was just not going to work.

My phone rang. I grabbed it off the edge of the couch and answered, "Hello?"

"How's the bun in the oven?" Creole asked me.

That was when I started crying and blurted out, "I think he's cheating on me."

"Damn!"

I took a deep breath. I knew all the things he was showing me. His disregard for his household, not coming home like he used to, and not wanting to have sex with me were signs of cheating. And if he wasn't cheating, then maybe he was falling out of love with me, which hurt as much as cheating, because if he plain out didn't want me anymore, that meant I would lose him. I was so confused as to what to do about the situation.

"What is he doing differently to make you think that, L?"

"He's coming home late, talking about how he had to work late four nights in a row this week. It was the same thing last week. He stayed late three days. And the week before it was two days. He has this funky-ass attitude toward me, finding any and every reason to start an argument with me. And he acts like he doesn't want me to touch his black ass."

"What are you going to do?"

Before I could reply, he walked in the house, swept past Sierra, who was watching cartoons, gave me a dirty look, and went into the bedroom.

His iciness toward me hurt. I loved him, and I was carrying his child.

"I'll call you back."

I patted Sierra on her head and walked past her to the bedroom, following after his ass. I stood in the doorway and watched him. He went straight to the shower. That was a new move.

Part of me felt he did so to wash away the scent of another woman. And a part of me prayed that he was just tired and sweaty from work and just wanted to freshen up and unwind with a warm shower. I prayed that all these things that I had interpreted as signs of estrangement were just figments of my imagination. But the logical side of me felt they weren't.

I waited as I heard the water running and him scrubbing himself. I didn't say nothing, though. Just listened. Ten minutes later I watched him come out of the bathroom with a towel wrapped around him and walk into the bedroom. I followed after him.

When he saw me standing there, he snapped, "What?"

"James, what's going on with you lately? You have had this snappy attitude. You're not keeping your word on the things you promised. You been coming home late, and you won't touch me anymore. It makes me feel like you're cheating on me."

When he started getting dressed, ignoring my questions, I started crying. "Can't you just answer me?"

"Baby, it's nothing. Since the other CPA quit, they are doubling up on my workload. I'm always tired, which is why I never bother with having sex anymore. I don't have the energy, and as a man, it would kill my ego if I didn't satisfy you the way you like. All you would get is a couple of humps. Then that would start more problems. Because you would feel I'm not trying to satisfy you. And then you forget this is tax season, so I been doing a lot of the employees' taxes for extra money, because when you go on maternity leave, I'm going to have to pay these bills in here. Everything doesn't have to be about another woman. All your pregnancy I have been spoiling you, but you want to focus of the last few months and make me this bad guy."

He did have a point. He had been good to me all this time. Why would he just change up out of the blue? Maybe it really was his job. I did know that his coworker had quit. He had told me that before

I started to feel bad, so I told him, "I'm sorry, baby. The last thing I want to do is add more stress to you." Now I really felt bad. "Are you hungry?"

"Naw. I grabbed something at work. Just let me sleep."

"Okay." I left the bedroom and went into the living room.

Chapter 18

All right, I know that I said I believed James. But I still had to be 100 percent sure he wasn't lying to me and seeing another woman. So the next day I dropped Sierra off at Greg's mother's house and went back home. Saturdays were supposed to be his night out with the boys, while I lounged at home. Only I didn't step foot in my house. What I did instead was park around the corner. Like clockwork, James's truck pulled up, and he hopped out and walked briskly into the house. I rushed up to his truck, used the spare key he had given me to open the hatchback, and jumped in back.

The truck had a third row of seats. I pushed those seats down and left the second row up so it would block any view of me. I waited in the truck for about fifteen minutes before he hopped back in. I lay on my side, with my legs crammed into my stomach. I hoped he'd hurry and get where he was going, 'cause my legs were getting cramped. It was a good thing James took pride in his truck and it wasn't packed with shit, like my bucket was. And with the cologne he wore, he did smell so fresh and so clean.

I held my breath until he started up the car. Then I breathed slowly.

He got on his cell. "Hey, baby. I'm on the way. Make sure you ready this time."

This time?

My head was banging against the inside of the truck, and he was playing Dwele. I knew he had snatched my damn CD. I had asked him if he took it, and he'd said no. *Lying bastard. You lie about a CD, so who knows what else you'll lie about?* Shit, CDs cost only fourteen dollars, five if they were bootleg.

I knew he had hopped on the freeway, because he was going fast as hell. Minutes later he coasted down a street, singing, "For the weekend, baby." After another couple of minutes he brought the truck to a stop.

I leaned up a little bit, peeked, and saw someone get in the passenger seat.

"Hey, baby." That was him.

My heart sped up.

"Hey, sexy." That was him again.

I heard smacking and more smacking and more smacking.

"Slow down, baby." That was a chick.

"Well, shit, what did you expect, wearing that little-ass dress you got on?"

"Well, I wanna go to the movies," she whined.

"Well, I want some pussy."

She started giggling, and he joined her.

"James, you so silly." Her voice turned serious. "But you are taking me to the movies."

"Well, let me eat your pussy."

And *this* was what had fathered my baby. I was so disgusted. I wondered how many times he had tasted her pussy and come home and kissed me on the lips. He was tainted, and I was so disappointed in him.

"Okay, damn. Hurry up, and don't get my panties messy like last time."

I lifted myself up farther and watched him slide his seat back. I slid a little closer 'cause it was dark, and I made her out. She was positioning her legs so he could go down on her.

When she leaned over to lift her panties off, I got a really good glimpse of the funny-looking bitch. She wasn't even cute, not by far, and she had a fucked-up weave.

When I saw his head dip between her thighs, I sat all the way up so they could see me. "James!"

The chick screamed and jumped in her seat. I wondered if she knew about me.

"Shit!" he yelled and pulled away from her.

I pressed the handle on the hatchback door so it slid up. Slowly lowering my feet to the ground as best I could so I didn't fall or bump the baby, I got myself out of the back of the truck.

The doors of the truck opened, and she got out and backed away when she saw me. Then she eased towards her house.

James, however, ignored her and rushed up to me, his eyes wide, wiping his face. "Baby." He tried to grab my arm, but I snatched away from him. "Baby, listen!" He was sweating and breathing hard. Pussy was on his breath.

I pushed him with one hand and backhanded his ass with the other. "Fuck you, James. Fuck you."

I walked away and from the corner of my eye saw him hop back in his truck. Soon I heard his truck start up. I kept walking, shivering and crying as I went.

He drove alongside me and yelled out the window, "Baby, get in the car!"

I flipped him the bird and felt my heart caving in as tears and sobs came from me. I held one hand on my tummy and kept on walking.

He sped up. "Baby, get in this car!"

A car horn sounded, and I heard tires skid on the pavement as a car drove around him.

"Baby, you gonna get me killed out here!"

I ignored him again, then turned down a main street. We were in Palos Verdes. He followed me for a while, but I refused to get in his truck.

I pulled my cell phone out of my pocket and called Crystal and asked her to pick me up. I sat down at a bus stop and waited for her. James remained parked alongside the bus stop and waited until my sister arrived. Once she did he pulled off.

I cried all the way to my house.

Creole packed up all of James's shit, drove it to the house he shared with his brother, and dumped it on the porch. According to her, she told James as she did this, "You bitch-ass nigga, you step foot on my friend's property, I'll do you like Al Green's and Lionel Richie's wives did they ass. Try it if you want to, muthafucka! I'm connected!"

And to that he responded, "Tell my baby I'm sorry and I love her."

"Fuck you!" she yelled.

During the first couple days it was hard to fight the urge to talk to him, because I really did love him and miss him, despite the fact that I'd caught him red-handed giving face to another woman. That shit hurt me. I had thought he was really going to be serious, and instead he fucked up. I knew it was best that I not have anything to do with him anymore. He wasn't healthy for my sanity, because when I saw him in that truck with that bitch, I wanted to slice and dice them both.

So Creole became my bodyguard, dealing with him and helping me around the house and with Sierra. She showed him no mercy when he called. She would hang up on him, but then he would call me right back.

"She don't want to talk to you, fool!" she yelled one day, while I stared off into space.

I didn't even bother to strain my ears to hear what he said.

Creole took a deep breath and said from the kitchen, "Allure, do you wanna talk to this clown?"

"Tell him to leave me alone," was all I said.

"You heard that shit, punk-ass, bitch-ass, bum-ass nigga! Leave my girl the fuck alone before we get some grits and fish grease ready for your ass."

Moving on from this situation, I tried to concentrate on my last exams of the semester, and I tried to keep myself in good spirits so I didn't affect the baby. Talking to or thinking of James's ass and what he did definitely would not keep me in good spirits. I tried not to think about him, but it wasn't always that easy. My mind was occupied with Sierra, schoolwork, cooking, and cleaning, but in those small moments of downtime I had right before I lay down, he always came to mind. He had hurt me yet again. Left more scars on me.

And I was now alone, because I refused to be with a lying-ass cheater. I would sit and cry, despite the fact that I knew it wasn't good for the baby. Negative thoughts weren't all that consumed me in those moments. I missed James—the way he held me when it was good, the way he made love to me, how he told me how pretty I was when I felt like a fat ass, how he would take the time to make sure Sierra was okay. Every night he would go into her room and make sure the covers were on her. I missed those things, his overall presence, even when he stopped being so considerate, because I loved him.

Each day that went by, things got better. The strain on my heart was less. I tried to smile. And get excited about my baby.

Two weeks before my due date we had my baby shower. James and I had wanted it to be coed. But since we had broken up, I didn't expect his friends to show up, but a few of them actually did. They dropped off gifts for me and left.

The shower was a lot of fun. My sister, Creole, and Kendra took care of everything. Sierra was the little helper. She passed out clothing pins, and any time someone crossed their legs, she collected the clothing pin from them. She giggled every time she caught someone. All I had to do was sit, relax, and eat. My mother cooked everything. There were pans of lasagna, barbecue, lemon-pepper chicken wings, pasta salad, Texas toast, and chocolate fondue with strawberries. Yummy! Everything looked so good. So while everyone played all the baby shower games, like finding the safety pins in the rice and guessing how much candy was in the bottle or what type of candy was in the diaper—I personally hated the diaper game—I grubbed down, having a really good time.

"Okay, it's time for the tissue game. Allure, get your fat ass up," Creole said. She brought a roll of toilet tissue, and I stood so Kendra could wrap it around my waist. The goal of the game was for the guests to guess how many squares of tissue were wrapped around my stomach.

I laughed at Kendra as she wrapped the tissue around my bulging belly.

"Damn," she joked. "This bad boy is going to split you wide open."

"A bust-it baby!" Creole joked.

I continued to laugh.

When Kendra had the squares of tissue wrapped around me, I stood still while people wrote down their guesses.

Suddenly my sister walked up to me with a frown on her face.

"What's wrong?" I asked her.

Before she could respond, the living room door burst open and James walked through it.

As he took steps toward me, I paused. Kendra unwrapped the tissue from my stomach.

"What the fuck is he doing here?" Creole said under her breath.

I ran a hand across my face and looked him over. He was wearing a white T-shirt, a pair of basketball shorts, and a pair of Jordans. His hair was disheveled, and it looked like he hadn't shaved. He didn't look like the normal clean and neat James I knew. I wondered if he looked this way because of our breakup. Did he really feel that strongly for me? I wondered. Then I wondered if he truly did, why he jeopardized that by messing with another woman.

When he stood in front of me, I demanded, "What are you doing here, James?"

Instantly tears streamed down his cheeks, turning everyone's attention in the room on him.

Before I could say anything else, he gushed out, "This month without you has been like dying. I'm sorry, baby. I don't know what I was thinking. I got scared, and my midlife crisis came early in my life and was fucking with me. Will you please forgive me?" Before I could reply, he fell to his knees and hugged my belly, smearing his tears and rubbing snot-stained face on my pretty, hot pink, baby-doll maternity dress. My favorite one.

"James." But as I said this, I instantly felt my icy heart soften toward him.

"And I brought you this." He pulled away momentarily and took something out of his pocket, a small box. He popped it open. Inside was a shiny diamond ring.

I gasped. He was about to propose to me.

But that wasn't the only reason why I gasped. Just as he slid the ring on my finger, fluid suddenly gushed out of me and ran down my legs. My water had broken.

James saw it too. His eyes got buck wide.

My sister screamed, "Allure! Mama!"

My mom came out of the kitchen. "What is it?"

James said, "She's going into labor. I'll take her to the hospital."

"Allure, are you sure?" my sister asked.

As much as James had hurt me, I couldn't deny him seeing the birth of his first child. I just couldn't. I knew it probably made me look weak to my family and friends. But I would just have to look that way. So I said quickly, "It's fine. But I want you guys there, too, if you can."

"I'll stay here with Sierra," Creole offered. "Fuck that. Call me when you pop that sucka out."

"I'll come," Kendra said.

James grabbed me by one of my hands and rushed me to the door.

"Allure, we'll follow you over there. I'll bring your bag," my sister said.

Creole handed James my purse and gave him a look like he was walking shit. He ignored her.

"Come on, baby," he said.

I moaned as a contraction hit me. People were still talking to me. But as the cramp pulsated throughout my body, I tuned it all out.

Chapter 19

Once we got the emergency room at Community Hospital on Termino Avenue, James let me go momentarily to rush up to a nurse and yell, "My baby mama having my baby!"

I held my belly and kept moaning after another contraction.

The nurse gave him an odd look and quickly rushed off. She came back with a wheelchair. When she reached us, James helped me into the chair, and I was wheeled off to the labor and delivery ward.

As soon as we got there, I was placed on a bed.

James was all in my face. "You gonna be okay, baby."

I was in a whole lot of pain, and I was not going to have the baby naturally. James looked at me tenderly. I looked the other way. "Just get the doctor and tell him to shoot me up with something! Something! Something!" I yelled.

"Baby, you don't wanna have it natural?"

"Medicine!" I screamed.

The nurse rushed back in and stripped me out of my dress. She put a gown on me and hooked me up to an IV. They inserted something in it, and I was soon in la-la land, only to wake up again when I was hit by another contraction. I wasted no time asking for the epidural.

***

Jeremiah . . . That was what I named him. I didn't give much thought to the names in the book I had read. As soon as I saw his little face, that was the name that came to me for my little cutie-pie. I counted his toes, his little fingers; looked in his eyes, which he was trying his best to keep open; inspected his tongue; let him smell me, his mama. I let him blow his sweet breath on me, let him try to suck my nose right off of my face. Hugged him to my chest close, cried those same tears I cried when I was able to hold my sweet Sierra for the first time. Then, when my arms were getting too loose and too weak to hold him, I handed him to his daddy, who held him up proudly. Then he was ever so gently snatched away by Creole, who looked at James like he was shit again.

"Can I hold my grandchild please?" my mom asked impatiently.

My mom, Crystal, and Kendra all got their moment with my little Jeremiah. Then, 'cause my work was all done, I went back on to sleep. Hell, with all that pushing I had done, I deserved it.

When it was time to bring the baby home, James wanted to accompany us and I let him. I loved him, and I wanted him with me to enjoy these precious moments. I didn't want to be done with him. Even if that wasn't the best choice to make. I was willing to take another chance on him, hoping that he didn't hurt me again. And I kept the engagement ring on my finger. I had never officially told him yes, but I hadn't said no. I wanted to see if he turned himself around after that bullshit. I even let him move his stuff back in. He was so happy about the new baby. He went crazy, buying him all the new Jordans, which, of course, he couldn't fit into. "My son's gonna represent," he said. I thought it was cute how he doted on Jeremiah.

Little Jeremiah was keeping us both up at night, that was for sure. And he slept like an angel during the day. I was hoping I would get lucky like I was with Sierra, in the sense that after the first couple months, Jeremiah would adapt to a regular sleeping pattern.

My family was definitely there to support me with the new baby.

"So are you sure you can trust that fool?"

I stared at my sister, Crystal, and Creole. Creole was the one who'd asked me that question. They had come over to see the baby.

Crystal was holding little Jeremiah, and I was putting pigtails in Sierra's hair.

"Hurry, Mommy."

I laughed. "Okay."

She was anxious for me to finish her hair so that she could lie near Jeremiah and look at him.

I put a barrette on one of her pigtails. "To tell you the truth, Creole, I really don't know. He said things would be different now."

"Well, have they been?" Creole asked.

"He's home. He gave me this ring. And he's looking for a home for us."

"Make sure your name is on that home, too, Allure." My sister said.

I nodded.

"I mean, if he decides to do right, that would be so good for you, because you been through enough," Crystal said. "You don't need any more heartache. You need to finish school. You're almost done, and now you got an extra mouth to feed. You don't need any more distractions."

And I hadn't planned on having another baby while I was finishing school. James had admitted to me that that night in San Diego he didn't put on a condom, so this shit was partly his fault—and fully my fault. Mine for trusting his ass. But every time I looked at little Jeremiah's face, I couldn't be angry with James. Little Jeremiah was far too precious to regret. I never saw a child as a mistake. But had I mentioned that part of the equation to my sister, Kendra, and Creole, they would hate James a whole more than they already did. But I forgave James for all his bullshit and hoped there was no more to come. I loved my kids, and I loved him. I wanted us to stay a family. I didn't want to raise my son without his father. Sierra was also attached to James. So I was quiet, and I nodded again.

"And he has such a beautiful family," Crystal said.

"Let that fool mess up this time . . . ," Creole said. "Sierra, cover your ears." Once she did, Creole said, "'Cause I got something for his ass if he does. That something just got out the pen."

We all laughed at Creole.

Everything was going so well for me. Greg and I had even been able to get along. Sierra was still going to his mother's house on the weekends. I didn't know how long it would last, this peace between him and me, but I enjoyed having less stress and fewer headaches from him.

Just then James walked in the door. He was greeted with silence. I knew I couldn't make my sister and Creole like him. He had brought that shit on himself. If it were my sister or Creole, and a guy had done to them what James had done to me, I would feel the same way. I knew that how they felt was completely normal. He had done me wrong, and they wanted me to be with a man who treated me well. I was sure that if he did right from this point forward, their feelings toward him would change. He didn't bother speaking to anybody. He yanked one of Sierra's pigtails, leaned over and kissed me, and took Jeremiah out of Crystal's arms. Then he went into the bedroom and didn't come back out until my guests had left.

That summer I didn't go to summer school so I could bond with Jeremiah. I spoke to my counselor, and he said I could still graduate on time. I didn't have to worry about studying or running to class. I could stay home and get properly acquainted with my baby. He was now six weeks old. James seemed to be coming around slowly in terms of what his role was. He didn't give me any indication that he was being unfaithful and was just being slick about it. I guessed that if he was doing something, he was really keeping the shit tucked under the covers. And the good moments never wavered between James and me. We did the family thing, and he even found the time to take me out on Fridays. We would go to Dave & Busters, to concerts, and even to an occasional club.

He had another surprise for me when we went house shopping.

"Do you like this one, baby?" he asked. It was in Lakewood.

I walked around the big three-bedroom house, holding Jeremiah in my arms, while James held Sierra's hand. We followed the real estate agent.

"It's nice. What do you think, Sierra?"

She smiled, making her right dimple poke out of her cheek. "Ummm, does it have a backyard?"

"Yeah, let's go see it." James threw her on his back, and they went out to the back.

I cradled Jeremiah in my arms, thinking it would be a dream to have a house like this for my kids and me. I finally felt like God was blessing me. I had a man who loved me, two healthy kids, and I was almost done with school. What else could I ask for?

When we got home from house hunting, I went into the kitchen to take out the ground beef for the meat loaf I was going to make.

James came up behind me and wrapped his arms around my waist and kissed me on my neck. "Let me do dinner tonight, baby."

I chuckled. "What are you gonna make?" I liked that he was being so considerate, because I didn't feel like cooking.

"Let me surprise you."

He rubbed his dick against my ass.

I chuckled. I was just as horny as he was. He knew the last week of my abstinence had passed and I could be intimate again.

"I'll be back, baby." He grabbed his keys and dashed out the door.

Because it was kind of late and James was taking longer than I expected, I fed Sierra a TV dinner so her little behind could go on to bed. Then I fed little Jeremiah my titty and burped him so his little butt would go to sleep too.

By the time James came home with Outback, I was buck ass naked. My six weeks was officially up, and I could get me some.

"Baby, Sierra, the food is here," he called.

I tiptoed from my room, past the living room, and into the kitchen and slipped behind him. I let my tongue glide down his neck.

He froze.

"We can eat that later." I turned him around so he could see my naked ass.

His eyes widened, and he burst into a smile.

I turned around and walked into the bedroom we shared, and he followed behind me like a puppy. Once there, I lay on the bed and split my legs open.

"Baby, I been waiting for this moment for so damn long," he said.

I laughed when he leaped on the bed as I lay on my back with my legs thrown in the air. He started kissing me all over my body. Wet kisses, making me moan.

Between kissing and groping me, he said, "Baby, I want you to know that I been one hundred percent faithful. That's why I'm about to bust, waiting for your pussy to heal."

I shivered and moaned when he put his tongue on my nipples.

I shoved him off of me and went to the dresser and bent over so my ass was all up in his face.

"Come get this, then, and stop playing," I said.

He massaged my butt cheeks, stuck his fingers in my pussy until it was wet and just right for him. He then started eating me out from behind, driving me crazy. I became so weak that I almost fell. James carried me back to the bed and laid me down. I watched him put on a condom. Then he mounted me and slid his dick into my long-awaited and tight-as-hell pussy. It hurt a little at first as it stretched to accommodate his dick. He flipped me over so that he could hit it from the back.

I moaned as he slapped my ass, making my cheeks jiggle. *Thank you, Jeremiah, for giving your mama some ass!* I thought. Finally, I had some rump. Who would have known I'd get it with my second baby?

I moaned again as he swiftly entered me and excited me. It had to be good to him, too, 'cause he was damn near choking, and slobber was dripping onto my back, but I didn't care.

"That feels so good, James!"

He flipped onto his back and let me ride him.

I was surprised to see tears coming out of his eyes.

"I love you, baby. I love you. Allure, I'm gonna be so good to you. I'm gonna do you right this time, baby!" He groaned loudly, and before he could stop himself, he came.

I lay down on his chest. We both took a minute to catch our breath. James went into the bathroom. I heard water running and knew he was cleaning himself up. He came out and lay back on the bed.

I peeked at Jeremiah's sleeping face in the crib. Then I looked at his father. He was lying on the bed like he was king of the damn world.

I crawled over to him and took his dick in my mouth.

James moaned instantly and said, "Damn, baby. Like that?"

I licked all around the circumference of his dick, before deep throating him again.

He groaned, and I shushed him. "Don't wake up Jeremiah, or *you'll* be up with him."

"Sorry, baby."

I used my hands to stroke up and down his dick in quick movements. Then I licked between strokes until he was shaking. I placed a hand over his mouth when I squeezed my lips together because I didn't want him to yell and wake the baby.

When his cum busted out from his dick, I took it. I swallowed it like it was a smoothie.

He threw his head back and said, "Man, I love you, Allure."

I just laughed and got comfortable in his arms.

***

Later that night we talked.

"Listen, I know I made a lot of mistakes, but I am so happy you gave me another chance to make things right, Allure."

He traced the shape of my lips with his finger before kissing me.

I smiled.

"I'd be a damn fool, giving up a woman like you. You are the best thing that ever happened to me. I'm just glad I realized that in time. You helped me grow up and look at what is important in life. Being a man, being about my word. I always think when I look at Jeremiah, what if I didn't have the chance to be in Jeremiah's life?"

"Whether we are together or not, James, I'd still let you see your son. I'd never take that away from you."

He kissed my forehead. "That's why I love you so much. It's the kind of woman you are. You work so hard. You take good care of Sierra and now Jeremiah. You have always had a lot on your shoulders, and you keep it moving without much complaining. Most women couldn't handle all that you do, baby. Then it's other things about you I love. How you really make a big effort to please me. I may not always say it, but I see it. Half the time I don't know what the fuck I'm talking about, but you let me ride my point out without making me look stupid. You show me that you value me. You let me feel like a man. And you're just so sweet. I see a lot of you in Sierra too. I can't believe nobody snatched you up before I got you. I see why your baby father damn near lost his mind over you. I'd bet he'd do anything he could to get you back."

But would you? I thought. *If you see all good, just give that good back by just loving me and doing right by us. That's all I ask.* I didn't need anything else but this, what he was giving me now. The way it was now was certainly good enough for me.

"This is all I ever wanted, James. A home and a healthy environment for my daughter and son. And to be loved."

"You don't ask for much."

"So if you know that, then you know to do right."

"Baby, I am. Like I said, I'm fortunate you even bother to fool with me. You, Sierra, and Jeremiah, y'all three are blessings. I can't say that enough."

I kissed him slowly, using my tongue.

"Don't get me started again," he murmured.

He ended up making love to me again. This time I cried, because I believed James really loved me in that moment and that he really wanted to be here.

When I woke up the next morning, James kissed me on my lips and grabbed one of my bared titties. Then he whispered, "Last night was good, baby. Real good. You know I want some more of that when I come home today, right?"

I smiled.

"Look at you, still bashful." He gave me a wink and grabbed his jacket. "Give Jeremiah and Sierra a kiss for me. I'm running late."

"Okay."

Jeremiah must still be knocked out, because I didn't hear a peep from him. I got up and searched for my robe. I wanted to put it on just in case Sierra ran into the room. I didn't want her to see me in my birthday suit.

When I didn't see it, I instead grabbed James's T-shirt that was lying on the floor near the bed. I slipped it on.

"Sierra!" I called.

"Coming, Mommy!"

I tiptoed over to Jeremiah's crib, not wanting to wake him if he was asleep but wanting to get a peek at my baby. It was always exciting to wake up each day to my new baby. The feeling hadn't gone away yet.

I leaned over his crib and smiled at his cute little face. I rubbed one of my fingers along his feet under the blanket. They were cold. My eyes narrowed.

I pressed my face closer to his face so I could feel his breath on my cheek.

I didn't feel it. Something was wrong with my baby.

I placed my hand on his little chest, over his heart. It wasn't beating.

"Sierra!" I pulled Jeremiah from the crib. My baby still wasn't breathing.

Sierra came running into the room. "What's wrong, Mommy?"

"Call nine-one-one! Now!"

I laid my baby on the bed. With shaking hands, I used my two fingers to pump his heart, and I also gave my baby my breath, sobbing and screaming wildly as I did this, so loudly that Sierra ran from room.

A few seconds later I heard her tell someone, "We need help! Help my mommy!"

I screamed and continued to pump my baby's chest and breathe into his little mouth.

But I wasn't God, so I could not save someone who was already gone, and my baby was gone.

Chapter 20

SIDS. Sudden infant death syndrome. That was what killed my baby. My little Jeremiah died in his sleep. That was what made me hurt inside, made little Sierra cry that she lost her brother, and made James refuse to eat and find it hard to sleep. He had an even harder time at the funeral. Funny . . . you could experience joy for a moment, but then it got snatched away real quick, almost quicker than the joy came. That was something, because it could take a while for joy to come into your life. But there were no time periods in life where pain was void in coming.

There was nothing much that could be said to change what had happened. I appreciated my family's and friends' thoughtful wishes, but they wouldn't make little Jeremiah's heart beat again. It wasn't their fault that this was the case, so I smiled graciously and accepted the casseroles, cakes, and pies that piled up on the kitchen table, uneaten. I tried to find a way to be optimistic about life without Jeremiah in it, because I had no choice. Being down was not going to bring him back. It would just keep me down. And I still had Sierra. I had to smile for her. I had to give James that reassuring pat on the back and tell him that everything would be okay, that we'd get through this, even if the day before he snatched his back away. I was gonna always offer that comfort to him because I loved him, even if he didn't offer it to me. Eventually, he would feel like it was okay to feel again, okay to smile and laugh, even though little Jeremiah wasn't here. But neither of us would ever be the same. It just wasn't possible.

I dragged James with Sierra and me to a therapist that dealt with loss and grief. I thought it was a good idea for us to see her together.

"What are you going to miss about Jeremiah the most, Sierra?" the therapist asked her during our counseling appointment.

The whole time James sat there with a frown on his face. In fact, lately all he had was a frown on his face. A frown I couldn't take off, 'cause he wouldn't let me . . . in.

"I'm gonna miss the way he smelled always like baby powder and the way he sucked his thumb." She had a sad look in her eyes. It broke my heart. I tried my hardest not to cry. My hardest. "I'll even miss him when his diaper stinks, 'cause it used to stink, huh, Mommy?"

I laughed softly and looked at James.

He gave me a sharp look. "This is bullshit!" He jerked his body off the chair and rushed out of the room.

Before I could go after him, the therapist said, "Let him go, Allure."

So I did.

He refused to show up for our next appointment. When I confronted him, he had an attitude.

"That bitch ain't doing shit for us but bringing in an extra bill."

"She showing us how to deal with this, 'cause what you doing ain't helping, baby. You have to grieve. You holding it all in—"

"Bitch, don't give me that grieving shit."

My eyes widened. He had never, ever spoken to me that way before. He had never called me out my name or raised his voice at me. It hurt. I was going through pain too. But it was like he didn't see that this was killing me as well. All he was thinking about was himself. Part of me wondered if he blamed me for Jeremiah's death. Countless times I had placed the blame on myself. Wishing that I had checked on him sooner than I did. Maybe if I had, he would still be there. But the pain of losing him, the guilt, and the hatred James seemed to now have for me were just too much.

He refused to meet my shocked, hurt gaze. I turned my back on him, slipped into our bedroom, and closed the door behind me.

"I'm sorry, baby." Later that night James lay next to me in bed as I lay on my side. He was rubbing all over my body, but I didn't want sex. It was the last thing on my mind.

Still, I didn't fight him when he pulled my nightgown over my head and started kissing me so roughly, I couldn't breathe. I pulled away, but he was stronger and flipped me onto my stomach.

Before I could stop him, he jammed his dick in my pussy so roughly, I whimpered. I tried to pull away, but he gripped both my thighs and I ended up with my face buried in the mattress.

He slid out and pumped back in, using all his strength. He was hurting me. I couldn't believe he would treat me this way. And I accepted it like I deserved it. Like this was my punishment for Jeremiah dying. For James's pain.

I cried and gripped the comforter in my hands. He entered me sharply again, and I cried out in pain. Then he froze.

"What the hell am I doing?" He released my thighs and tried to hug me, but I snatched away from him and curled in a ball.

"I'm sorry, baby."

But the damage was done. I had been taken somewhere I had already been with Greg. This was something I had shared with James, and he had done me the same way. So his "sorry" couldn't do much to fix the situation.

He rose from the bed, pulled his pants back on, and left the room and the house. I didn't stop him.

He never came back. He left me and Sierra. A few days later his brother came to collect his things.

Following the breakup, James pretty much dropped off the face of the earth. No call, no show, no nothing. As if Sierra and I had never existed. Pride forced me not to call him, although I wanted to. I was so hurt. I mean, my son had died, and now the man that had vowed never to leave me or hurt me had. I knew I had to will myself to be done with him. He was no good for me. Truth was, I knew what I needed to do. I needed to remain alone, get back into the church, maybe even find a hobby. I handled all my responsibilities to a T. I was passing all my classes, going to work every day, and Sierra was safe, healthy, and well loved.

It seemed that no matter how busy and overwhelming my life got, there was still a void, this severely depressing feeling about being alone that seemed to be with me often. This void kept me up at night, crying and miserable. And I just couldn't ride it out. I felt I had to be with someone. To be honest, the turnaround time after James was really quick. I knew it was too soon, but I was lonely and desperately and wanted someone in my life. The time I spent with other men was when Sierra was with her father on the weekends. I even called Derek, hoping he would still have an interest in me. But he informed me that he now had a woman.

My mother wanted me to just take a break from men after what I had been through, but I chose not to listen. But what I did do was forbid myself from being so into one man, from sharing so much of myself, from showing my vulnerabilities.

I started seeing two men. One was named Andre. He was thirty and was an aspiring singer who worked as a cop. A cop! I was dating a man in blue. I met him on the job. I was speeding down the 710, and his ass got me, so it was either a ticket or his number. Happily, I took the latter, 'cause he wasn't bad looking. And I didn't exactly have 150 bucks to spare for the ticket. The other one's name was Bryce. He was a welder I met at the mall. He was a church boy who went faithfully every Sunday.

I hoped something came of one of these relationships. All I wanted was to feel like I was important to somebody. Find some way to get rid of this ache I was feeling inside. A good man was what I sought. No games, either. I needed to make sure that I was careful, that I protected my heart. I tried my best not to get attached to either one of these guys.

See, Bryce appealed to my sensibilities from a physical standpoint, and he was so laid back. Bryce would invite me over his house and cook me breakfast and flex, while Andre would sing a song to me that made me swoon and then talk to me about politics. About how it frustrated him that our black family structure had been so destroyed. So I kept them both around. As both relationships progressed, to tell the truth, I realized that I liked Bryce the best, and thus I spent the most time with him. Bryce had an edge. I was also more attracted to Bryce. He always looked neater and more clean-cut. Andre, on the other hand, often looked sloppy and was always sweating. The only time he looked neat was when he was in his police uniform. But he still sweated even with it on.

As I felt myself getting closer to Bryce, I knew I had to tread cautiously. And not fall in love too quickly. Not give all of myself, but make him earn me. Look at what had happened between James and me. The best way to avoid a repeat of that was not to put all my time into one guy. But for the moment, Bryce was doing it for me, which caused me to give him a little more of my time than I gave Andre. But it didn't stop Andre from constantly calling.

I smiled and stared at Bryce across the table. We were dining at M & M. I was seeing Bryce more and more every week. And it was going good as hell. We had spent the majority of our date talking about my past relationship with James. I knew I said it was better not to discuss my past, but I felt comfortable with Bryce.

"I like you a lot, Allure. And I can't believe somebody would do the shit that that fool James did to you. You are really something special. Just what I need."

"Wow, that's really sweet. How is it that no woman has been able to luck up on you?"

"These women nowadays are . . ." I smiled when he shook his head.

I laughed. "We not that bad," I said, disagreeing.

"Shiiit. A woman nowadays will get your number, call you, invite you over, fuck the shit out of you, send your black ass home, and never call you again. And then, when you get up the courage to call her, she acts like you bugging her."

I burst out laughing when he said that. 'Cause I had a friend like that: Creole.

A few minutes later the waiter took our order. I ordered the pork chops, rice, gravy and greens and he ordered the oxtails and rice. It was a good meal and with good company.

After dinner Bryce drove me home and walked me to my door. I knew he was going to try to be slick and get into my pants. So I was ready for him. I had been seeing Bryce for a couple months, and I thought it was too soon to go there.

My cell phone rang. I looked at the number. It was Andre. I didn't answer.

Bryce shoved me up against my door.

"Behave, Bryce."

"Don't wear that dress anymore." He started kissing me and said between kisses, "I been wanting to do this all day."

He managed to get in a couple more kisses before I pulled away and told him to go home. I turned to unlock my door.

He slapped me on my ass and said, "Damn, girl. You gonna make me fall in love with you."

I pecked his lips one more time.

"I like that you're making me wait, though. It shows you're a classy lady." He winked and walked down my porch steps.

"Good night." I watched him walked out of the gate.

Chapter 21

It was Friday, and I was anxious to start my weekend. Bryce had planned a whole romantic day for me on Saturday. First, he was treating me to lunch at Benihana. I'd told him I had always wanted to go there. Then he wanted to take me to Puddingstone in San Dimas. I had never been there before, but Creole said she had and that it was pretty romantic. She said each room had its own private Jacuzzi.

I picked up Sierra from the babysitter after work, I rushed over to my doctor's office to have a routine checkup. While Sierra stayed in their supervised children's area, I went into an examining room. I gave urine samples and took an iron test where they plucked a little blood from my finger.

As I waited for my doctor to come in, I texted back and forth with Bryce.

Can't wait to see you on Saturday, he texted.
Same here. ☺, I texted.
I got you something pretty to wear.

I was about to text him, Blushing, but another text came through before I could. I opened it quickly, expecting it to be from Bryce, and was surprised as hell when I saw it was from James. It read, Miss you.

Before I had a chance to respond, someone walked into the room.

It was an older white lady whom I had never seen before. But I knew she had to be a doctor, because she had a white jacket on and she had a clipboard in her hand. Since I was anxious to get out of there, I didn't trip on needing to see my doctor. Anyone would do for me. Damn, James had texted me. *Wow.* I hadn't heard from him or seen him in a couple months.

"Allure Jones," she said, sitting on the stool, breaking into my thoughts.

"Yeah. I'm just here for—"

"How long have you been HIV-positive?"

"What?"

Okay, that was when the room started spinning. Her lips were moving, but I wasn't hearing her. That was when my heart started pumping a mile a second, when sweat and tears came out of my body and my legs felt like Jell-O, when my whole body—my head, neck, shoulders, arms, hands, legs, knees—was shaking, making it hard for me to hold myself up, and when I started screaming at the top of my lungs.

"Calm down, Ms. Jones."

Screaming and backing away from her, I spun around and didn't see the door in time. It swung open and knocked me upside my head. I felt even weaker now, and then I hit the floor and slipped into unconsciousness.

When I came to, I blinked a couple times, until my eyes focused. I moaned when they did 'cause I was still there, in that damn doctor's office, in that room where I had received the horrible news that my life was over and that I was going to die of AIDS. What would I say to my family? To little Sierra? She's going to have to see her mother sick.

I wiped fresh tears away. Touched the bandage on my forehead. Underneath it was a big knot. Probably to stop my blood, which was tainted blood, blood that had AIDS in it.

I bawled.

Someone knocked on the door. I didn't respond, so the person slowly slipped into the room. It was a nurse. The same one that had received me earlier. I guess she stepped into the room slowly because she knew I had the virus. Maybe she didn't want to get close to me.

She smiled at me. Wow. She wasn't this nice when I first walked in.

"Allure, hi. I'm Janet. I was the nurse that received you."

I knew who Janet was. I had been coming to that office for years. She was probably trudging slowly because she, too, knew my test results. So I nodded and stared out the window, feeling more tears pour from my eyes. My life was over. No one was going to want me now, and I damn sure couldn't have any more kids.

"Listen." She shook her head and came closer, so close that she grabbed both my hands. "I don't know how to tell you this."

I closed my eyes and sobbed, "I already know. I'm HIV-positive."

"No, you're not."

I froze. Then I turned around and faced her. "What did you say?"

She took a deep breath. "You're not HIV-positive, Allure. That crazy woman you saw lives on the street. She managed to get past security outside. She put on one of our jackets and snatched your chart, pretending she was a doctor. We had her arrested for breaking and entering. I'm so sorry for your distress."

"What? You mean to tell me that y'all dumb motherfuckers let a homeless bitch in here, and she had access to my business and life and told me I have AIDS?" I jumped from the examining table so fast that I lost my balance and fell on the floor. I jumped up again and snatched my purse from her. "Get the hell out of my way!"

I yanked the door open. I ran to the reception area. I knocked over all the paperwork on their front desk. Then I screamed, "You unprofessional muthafuckas!" while whipping around in a circle.

Silence was all I got. And a bunch of shocked expressions. From staff and patients.

"I'm suing the hell out of y'all, and by the time I'm done, you gonna have to shut this bitch down. So get ready."

I went over to the children's area to get Sierra. Unfortunately, she and the other kids over there had heard my rant.

"Mommy, what happened to you head?" she asked.

I ignored her question. "Come on."

We went home.

While I was at the doctor's, Bryce had called me on my cell phone and on my home phone. I didn't return Bryce's calls. I wanted the swelling on my head to go down before I saw him again. So I kept putting ice on the egg on my damn forehead. But truth be told, I did talk shit about suing them, but I wasn't going to. It was a mistake. A big one. Nonetheless, they didn't do it on purpose. I would rather have ten knots on my head than really have HIV. That was some scary-ass shit. I really wanted to die when that crazy woman read those results to me, and I thought my life was pretty much over. Thank God it was an error on a psycho's part.

As Sierra sat at the kitchen table to do her homework, I asked her, "What do you want for dinner?"

"Cookies!"

"How about some chicken fingers, potato salad, and string beans?"

"Yeah, that sound good, Mommy. But can we make cookies for dessert?"

I checked the cabinet to see if we had all the ingredients to make them. We had everything, down to half a package of chocolate chips. When I was a kid, I always loved to bake goodies, so Sierra and I often made cakes, pies, cookies, and whatnot together.

"Yeah, we can. Hurry and finish your homework."

"Okay."

She finished her work quickly, and I scanned it while the chicken fingers were frying. Then I let Sierra help me with the potato salad.

"Mama, you still didn't tell me what happened to your head," she said. I let her crack open the cooled boiled eggs.

"The door bumped into me," I joked and kissed her on her cheek.

She laughed and said, "Mommy, doors don't bump into people. People bump into them!" She had a little hand up when she made that statement.

I shook my head at her. "Sierra, remind me to stop paying the babysitter."

"No, Mommy!" she exclaimed, giggling. That girl loved her some La La.

"Then hush up and finish them eggs, girl." I was only kidding with her, and she knew it. So she kept on doing the eggs.

And, man, when we ate, you would have thought I was eating lobster bisque. That was how good the food tasted to me. It tasted good because I was okay. I didn't have a life-threatening disease.

After dinner Sierra and I whipped together some chocolate chip cookies. As they baked, I gave her a quick bath.

As soon as she was asleep, I was going to give Bryce a call and cancel our date for tomorrow. "Seems like you're ready. Girl, are you ready to go all the way?" I sang.

Sierra giggled at me.

"What you laughing at?"

"You, Mommy, 'cause when you sing, you sound bad."

I cracked up laughing and swatted her little bottom. Then I held up a towel for her. "Go on and dry off. Put on your nightgown. I'm gonna get the cookies out. They should be done by now."

She dashed off to her room.

I went into the kitchen to check on the cookies. They were done. I took them out of the oven, then let them cool down for about a minute. I poured two glasses of milk, one for Sierra and one for me, and placed the cookies on a plate. Then I joined Sierra, who was now sitting on the couch. We enjoyed the cookies and milk while watching *The Suite Life of Zack & Cody*.

When it was a little after eight, I told Sierra it was time to go to bed.

Once I had Sierra hidden under her Barbie covers and her damn near dozen pillows, she turned to me and said, "Mommy, I wanna tell you something but don't want to make you sad."

"What?"

"I miss Jeremiah, Mommy, all the time."

I gave her a smile. The best smile I could muster. I tried not to look sad. "I miss Jeremiah, too, Sierra. In fact, there's not a day that goes by that I don't think about him."

"Do you think he misses us?"

I ran my finger along her right cheek. "I know he does." I turned my back quickly so she didn't see my tears. I brushed them off of my face, then turned back to her. "We just have to appreciate the time God gave us with him and know that Jeremiah is in a better place."

"In heaven, I know."

"Yes, that's where he is."

I rose, but she said, "Mommy?"

"What, baby?"

"I miss James, too, but I didn't want to say that, 'cause that probably wouldn't make you sad. It probably would make you mad."

That was when I laughed. Yes, thoughts of James would make me angry, because he did us dirty. It was not something I wanted to make a habit of doing, telling my daughter that someone she had grown attached to was not coming back. I mean, she kept a brave face when I told her, but I knew deep down it hurt. And before he left, he vented a lot of his anger and snapped at me in front of Sierra. I thought we were both taking big steps by moving past James. I was glad we could joke about it. Part of me still pondered over his random text, which I never responded to.

"Go to bed, baby."

She pointed at the Strawberry Shortcake clock on the wall across from her bed. "But I still have ten minutes. Can I watch TV until eight thirty?"

"Girl, go ahead, but as soon as the big hand hits that six, you better get your little butt up and turn it off."

"Okay!"

I closed the door behind me, went into the living room.

I sat on the couch, thinking about little Jeremiah. A little sadness swept over me. I missed the hell out of my son. This made me forget what I was about to do, which was call Bryce. I told myself silently to get myself together and hummed the song I was humming earlier to break the mood I was now in. But I couldn't, so I decided against calling Bryce. Instead, I looked through my photo album at the pictures of Jeremiah, James, Sierra, and me. I couldn't help but shed fresh tears. I still couldn't understand why Jeremiah was taken away from me. I sat the photo album aside and closed my eyes as more warm tears slipped down my cheeks.

Just then my cordless phone rang. It was a blocked number. Curious, I answered. "Hello?" I said. I knew I sounded depressed.

"Hey. It's Andre."

Shit. I wished I hadn't answered. It wasn't that I didn't like Andre. I just liked Bryce more. Our vibe was better, and we had better conversations. It was like that sometimes. Calling me from a blocked number because I wouldn't answer when he called from his regular number made Andre look desperate. It made him look like he was jocking me.

"I called you a couple times today and even texted you," he said.

"I'm sorry. I was so busy today."

"Really? What did you do?"

I huffed out a deep breath into the phone. "Went to work, school, picked up my daughter from school, cooked dinner."

"Yeah? What did you make?"

I rolled my eyes. He was not going to let me get off this phone. "Chicken fingers," I told him, leaving everything else out.

"Oh, that sounds good. I went out to eat at P.F. Chang's."

"Really?" I said, not interested. I looked at the clock on the wall. It was eight thirty-five.

Sierra still had the TV on, on full blast. Just as I was about to tell her to turn it off, I heard a bang. It sounded like wood cracking. I saw that somebody had kicked my living room door in!

I jumped to my feet and screamed as a man rushed up in my house, and I screamed even louder when I realized that the man was Bryce.

"Bryce, what the fuck is wrong with you?" I backed up fearfully.

He rushed up to me and was so close, I had to back up more, until I felt the bottom rim of the couch against my ankles. I could hear Andre yelling my name on the phone.

Bryce snatched the phone out of my hand before I could say anything more to him. I closed my eyes briefly as he hung up and tossed the phone.

"Real talk. You got something to tell me?"

"What are you talking about?" I screamed. Looking at my exploded door, I hoped Sierra would stay in her room. I eased over so he wasn't so in my face. And as soon as I had a foot of separation between us, my instincts told me to run.

He stepped to me swiftly, as if sensing my impending flight, and before I could move again, he hauled off and slapped me upside my mouth. His ring tore through my skin. I fell to the floor and screamed.

"Bitch, I heard you was a man!"

"What?" I held my bleeding mouth.

He snatched me by my hair so I was now standing. I struggled against him. "Please don't hurt me," I begged.

"Bitch, I'm gonna kill you if what I heard is true."

"I'm not a man."

I knew there was no chance that I'd be able to fight this six-foot-four man, and I couldn't get to the phone, because he wouldn't let go of my neck. I tried to stay as still as possible, out of fear that any resistance on my part would cause him to hurt me. I prayed, *Please, God, don't let Sierra come in here and see this.* And I even prayed that Andre would come help me.

I almost peed on myself when another dude came through the door. *What are they going to do to me?* I thought. I feared that they would rape me or even kill me.

This dude peered at me, looked me up and down, all over my face and body, as if he was trying to figure out something.

Bryce was sweating and his eyes were searing into mine when he whispered, "Well, are you gonna come clean, bitch, or what?" Damn! This was not the man I had become acquainted with over the past two months. He was like a completely different person.

"I'm not a man."

He punched me in my stomach like I was a man. I moaned inwardly and slumped over a bit. The punch he gave me caused me to have a hard as hell time breathing. His hands went back to my neck. And he started choking me again.

I sobbed silently. I should have never invited him to my home. I called out to God again. *Please get me out of this.*

His friend continued to look at me up and down.

"Well, are you going to show me this shit ain't true or what, Allure? 'Cause I'm really starting to feel like it's true each fucking second that goes by."

"I have a daughter!"

"That don't mean shit. You probably lied about that shit."

His hold tightened.

Why would he think some shit like this? That I was a man? It was all too crazy to digest. But the hateful look on his face told me that he really felt it was true.

"Now, I'm gonna ask you one more time."

"I swear—"

"Man, fuck this shit."

He punched me again, hit my nose. I felt blood gush out of it. I hit the floor again. I bit my lip to keep from crying out.

"Get her legs, Ace!"

I lay helpless as his friend grabbed my legs and Bryce straddled me and ripped my shirt to shreds and pulled my bra off of my titties. For a moment Bryce looked like he was convinced, and a look of relief and guilt washed over his face, but his friend said, "That don't mean shit. Them hormones make they titties big. Check to see if she got a pussy, man."

Bryce had that crazy look in his eyes again. He held my arms in a death lock, so tight I thought some bones were gonna break. Then his friend pulled off my sweats and my panties.

"Police! Get your fucking hands up! Get your fucking hands up!"

It was Andre, with his gun drawn. Two more cops raced into the house.

Andre said, "Place your hands on your head. Lace your fingers. Get on your knees!"

I pulled my pants and bra back on and turned over on my stomach and sobbed uncontrollably.

I heard the cuffs being snapped on their wrists and their footsteps as they left my house. But I wouldn't look. I wrapped the shreds of my shirt around me, and I stayed rooted in the spot I was in.

Soon a blanket was thrown over me. I looked up and made eye contact with Andre.

Chapter 22

Thank God that I had answered when Andre called and that he'd come to my rescue.

Talk about a crazy-ass night. I was attacked by a man I was a day away from giving my pussy to. He had beat my ass and could have possibly killed me. Who would have thought he would be the type of man who could do some shit like that? But then I realized that two months was not enough time to know what type of man Bryce was. And I still had not been able to figure out where he got the crazy notion that I was a man. It was the craziest shit I had ever heard. I knew that I would drive myself crazy trying to figure it out. So I left it alone and thanked God that Sierra didn't see any of that. Part of the reason was that I let her keep the TV on in her room, which offset the noise in the living room.

That night I called my sister and my mom. They both rushed over. My mother went to the hospital with me, and my sister waited at home with Sierra.

Andre came to my hospital bed and took a statement from me. It felt awkward to tell him that I was seeing Bryce. But he kept all judgments off of his face and jotted everything down. He had on regular clothes. I assumed that was because he had been at home and had just rushed out to save me.

"Are you sure you're going to be okay, Allure?" It was Andre. Again I thought, *What a relief that he came.*

I nodded. "I think so." I grimaced because it was painful to talk. "Andre?"

He turned back around and faced me.

I took a deep breath. "Are you?"

He slipped a hand under my chin. "Mad?"

I nodded again and tried to turn away. I knew I looked ugly as hell. He held my chin firmly.

"No. Me and you didn't have a commitment. So as much as I would like to be angry, I don't have a right to. But I have to admit, I am a little jealous."

I stared into his light brown eyes and offered the best smile I could from the hospital bed. Old boy had fractured my nose, busted my lip, and my right eye was swollen shut. And I had to get stitches near my mouth, where his ring cut me.

"The nerve of him, treating a woman like you that way."

I touched my swollen lip, and my eyes teared up again.

"Don't worry about that. It will heal in no time." He sighed. "Well, I need to go and file this report. I'm going to also file for an emergency restraining order."

"Right."

"I will be calling you soon, most definitely."

"Thank you, Andre."

"Take care, Allure."

He gave one last wave before walking out of the room.

After my mother made it in to see me and asked her twenty-one questions about what happened to me and told me that I should have taken her advice and remained alone, I dozed off from the sedatives without answering a single one.

***

My stay at the hospital was three days long. I went home, but I didn't feel comfortable there anymore. I felt so violated. And for the first week, until I was able to adjust, either Kendra, my sister, or Creole spent the night. During this time I did a lot of talking on the phone to Andre.

It took about two weeks for the bruises to clear up. One scar remained, though. It would be a constant reminder of that night. Bryce ended up getting a year in prison for the assault, and the judge placed restraining order on him. He was not permitted to call me or come within one hundred feet of me. It was so crazy. I really thought he was a nice guy, but I didn't know him at all.

While I was healing, Andre and I got closer. One night in particular we had been on the phone for so damn long that my ear was packed with sweat. We had been talking for three hours straight.

"Are you bored yet?" I asked him. I was curled up on my couch, while Sierra was watching TV.

"I don't get bored talking to you, Allure."

"You know what? I don't either. You're a very interesting person, Andre." I wished I had given him a chance and had not got so caught up in Bryce. For me, Andre was as safe as they came. He was a police officer, for God's sake. Who could be more trustworthy?

When I heard a beep, I clicked over so I could hear my other line. "Hello?"

"Allure, don't hang up. This is Bryce."

My heart started pounding. How was he able to call me from prison? I thought. And why did he want to?

Before I could say anything, he said, "Listen, baby. I had my sister call you and place us on three-way. Just give me thirty seconds. I'm so sorry for what I did to you. And I'm paying for it with a year in prison. I deserve it for putting my hands on you. But it seems I had been given some misinformation. I have a brother. His name is Cedric. He works for the gas company as a construction worker. Anyway, the day we were texting each other back and forth, before I popped up at your crib, we were having a casual conversation, and I told him that I was seeing this young *tenda* named Allure. Well, he said that his boy Lavante used to fuck with someone named Allure and that you were bad news."

I gasped when he said Lavante's name.

"So naturally I was curious as to what it was that made you bad news. Because, like I said, I really liked you. And I wanted to make sure I wasn't wasting my time, in case you were a rat, a gold digger, and if that being the case I needed to keep it moving"

My heart started pounding fast.

"Well, that's when Lavante got on the phone and said that you were really a man."

I exhaled deeply. That piece of shit, that muthafucka was still trying to wreak havoc in my life. Maybe to him it was just a joke, a way for him to hate. But that shit could have got me killed. After all this time I couldn't believe he would say such a lie about me. I mean, it wasn't like I had done him wrong, and as a result, we broke up. He had misled me, hurt me, and I had moved on. How could he be so bitter about that and spread lies about me?

"Allure, is it possible that when I get out of here that we can—"

"No. But I do accept your apology."

"It's just that. Look, I flipped out because I was raped by my father when I was like ten. So the thought that I had been kissing and touching a man pretending to be a woman enraged me."

I wondered if it would have come out, this wee bit of information, if I had dated him longer. Or would it have continued to be a skeleton in his closet? And with him being damaged about it, what type of boyfriend would he have been to me? I was also confused. Was he a man who thought he had been tricked and reacted, or was he just a violent man? Then I figured there was no need to ponder this. He was something that didn't happen. And since things turned out the way they did, it wasn't meant to happen, either.

He could have simply asked me the truth, and if I had deceived him and had really been a man, he would have had the right to whip my ass. And I couldn't help but feel that he really was a broken man with deep issues, someone I didn't need in my life, so I was happy that things happened the way they did. Although I didn't enjoy the ass whipping, the truth had been revealed. Lavante was a lying-ass, hating-ass dick. And I knew he would have his day one day.

"Look, I don't mean to be insensitive, but you seem to have a lot of issues you may have not dealt with yet."

"Yeah. I'm thinking about getting counseling."

"You know what? I really think you should. You are a handsome and cool man. I really liked you and enjoyed being around you. But you ain't my problem to solve. And the fact of the matter is you assaulted me. I wouldn't be able to look at you in the same way. So the answer is no. Good luck."

Before I gave him a chance to respond, I hung up the phone. Maybe I was harsh, but that was the kindest I could be to him after what he did to me.

I had completely forgotten that Andre was on the other line. But I was too shaken up by what I had just learned to call him back.

***

I started spending more time with Andre. The weekend after I got that crazy phone call from Bryce, Andre took me on a date to the Santa Monica Pier. He had just got off work and came in his uniform. I knew it was a bit shallow of me to not give him as much of a chance in the beginning as I gave Bryce, because I was more attracted to Bryce. I was still a little grossed out by all the sweating, but Andre seemed like a nice guy. Maybe he had some type of condition that caused him to sweat. He always carried a small towel to clean his face.

As we walked and talked, he seemed to be so confused about the fact that I was still single. "So tell me this, Allure. Why is a woman like you on the market?"

Let's see, I thought. *Because the men that I have been with weren't shit. First, there was Greg, a psychopath. Then there was little dick Lavante. Let's get to James. . . . I don't know what to make of his ass. Then Bryce . . . That situation was another disaster. I can't catch a break for shit.*

But I simply replied, "Just haven't found the right person yet."

"Are the pickings that slim?" he asked me as we walked.

"Hell, yes. Think about it. A large number of black men are incarcerated, and what is left out there is gay or with nonblack women, or they are bum types of dudes. The cards seem to be stacked up against us. So what's a black woman to do?"

He laughed. "Don't believe the hype. There are plenty of good brothas."

I certainly hoped so. And I hoped Andre was one of them.

As we walked, people standing near and walking past stared at us. I had never gone anywhere with a man in blue. I felt special. Like I got a cop on me.

"You seem like you've been through a lot, Allure. I get that." He sat on a bench, then grasped my hand and pulled me down to sit on his lap.

Shit. I had learned one thing. It was not to share my past with a man. So I was wondering how I had let on about my troubles. I asked in a saucy manner, "How you figure that?"

He chuckled. "When you smile, Miss Feisty, it's not full. It tightens up. And I don't know. . . . There's a look you give. You look depressed."

I looked away as he wiped a thick layer of sweat off of his face.

"You're not supposed to talk about your past relationships," I said. But I was contradicting myself, because basically my tears confirmed his statement. "I been through some stuff that has changed me, changed my whole outlook, took away a little of my joy. That stuff doesn't allow me to feel as good as I can."

"Why?"

"Because I can't find a man to love me. Truly love me. Treat me right. To have that feeling, just know they really want to be there. For all the right reasons. I can't find it."

"Find what?"

"A soul to touch mine, be in sync with me, lift my daughter's heavy ass out the car when she falls asleep, unclog the sink when it gets stopped up, and really, really look at me and love at least ninety-five percent of me. Someone who will be decent to me. Who wants to grow with me and be there as much as I wanted him to. That's what I can't find. And it seems like such a minor thing that I'm asking for. Pure, wholesome, unconditional love."

He just stared at me for a long time. It looked like his eyes got a little watery.

"Allure, let that love find you and you can't go wrong."

"But in the meantime I'm lonely, and when I want to be held, kissed, and comforted, what do I do? And if it never comes, then what?"

He chuckled like he was on to something that I was not. "Baby girl, it already has. You just don't know it, and, girl, now that I found you, I'm not letting you go, that for sure."

I smiled, thinking, *I'm tainted. I don't fall for that shit no more. Promises. Go on with that shit.* But part of me still believed in all that romance shit, still believed that there were decent men out there looking for good women. That made me believe him, and it overpowered that tainted side of me.

I allowed him to hold me tight, and when I pulled away, I let him kiss me softly.

Chapter 23

Andre invited me over for dinner. I was flattered, but then warning signs went off in my head about going to his home. So far all the times we had hung out, we'd been in public places. Truthfully, I trusted Andre, but I still felt like I needed to be cautious. But he told me that his sister would be there, along with his friend and his friend's wife. So I thought, *Cool.* It made me feel a little important that he had invited me over to mingle with his sister and his friends. He had to be really serious about me if he wanted me to meet people in his world.

"Why don't you bring your daughter?" he suggested after our movie date. The dinner party was the next day.

"I haven't known you long enough for you to meet Sierra. Sorry. But she did say to tell you thank you for the Barbie doll you bought her."

I gave him a peck and slipped out of his patrol car. He always took me on dates in it. I didn't mind. In fact, it was exciting. He even did the sirens for me one day, and we ripped down the street. The only thing I didn't like about Andre was that he always tasted like cigarettes. He said he didn't smoke, but I knew he was lying. Because he always had this cigarette taste when he kissed me or I kissed him.

So the next day I got myself all pretty in preparation for dinner. To be honest, I was a little worried that he was already established and I wasn't. I was a twenty-four-year-old single parent. But I had goals I wanted to accomplish. I hoped the fact that I was in college and working was enough for his sister and his friends.

The dinner was on a weekday, so Crystal agreed to watch Sierra. The dinner didn't start until eight, and by that time Sierra would be in bed. I took my braids out, and my sister brought her gear to my home so she could wash, press, and flatiron my hair before putting a bunch of curls in it. It looked really nice.

My sister stood on my porch as I was leaving.

"Now, if anything goes down you not cool with, call me, Allure."

I nodded my head. Ever since that Bryce situation, my sister has been hella paranoid.

"You got my Taser gun, too, right?"

I laughed. "Yes, I do. But like I said, his sister, his friend, and his friend's wife will be there."

"All right, well, if anything goes down . . ."

"Crystal, I will be fine. Andre is a po-po."

"That don't mean shit! He could have a secret life."

"He's a cop, girl. I'll be okay."

"All right."

I walked out the gate and slipped into my car. She watched me from my porch steps.

When I got to Andre's house on the west side of Long Beach, before I could even knock, the door was thrust open and Andre gave me a bear hug. "Hey, baby!"

"Hey."

He looked me up and down. "You look nice. Come on in."

He grabbed me by my hand and led me into his living room. And to be honest, it was the most primitive-looking living room I had ever seen. It didn't make sense since he was a cop. I thought cops made a good salary.

There was one black suede couch, and a boom box sat in a corner of the room. A small TV sat on a plastic crate, and a picture of a bowl of fruit hung on the living room wall.

But hell, he was a bachelor, so maybe that was why it looked the way it did. Maybe it simply needed a woman's touch.

There was a woman sitting on his couch.

"Allure, this is my sister Wanda."

I walked closer to her. I held out my hand. "Hello."

She gave me a blank nod and rolled her eyes. She didn't shake my hand. *Half-dead-looking bitch,* I wanted to say, but I kept my smile pasted on and turned away, but not before I inspected her. The bitch looked tacky, anyway. She had on a faded red, oversized Nike shirt and a pair of pink leggings. Her hair was thin and greasy looking and had a pick comb in it.

"Where is your friend and his wife?" I asked.

"They haven't arrived yet." He ushered me into the dining room, which had a small table, the type you folded and took to picnics, and there were only two chairs. The dining room was attached to the kitchen, and only carpet divided it from the kitchen.

"Sit down, baby."

I sat and laid my purse on the table. I saw that his sister was still sitting in the living room, with the same expression on her face.

"I hope you like spaghetti."

"I do." I stood and walked in the kitchen. "You need some help?"

"Yeah, stir the spaghetti sauce. It's simmering. I'll be back." He rushed away.

I stirred the spoon in the little pan, which contained what looked like mostly sauce. I hoped he had some chicken to go with this shit, because it wasn't enough for five people.

Ten minutes later, when he came back into the kitchen, his face was wet with sweat. And his eyes were super dilated.

I was used to the sweat but not to his wide-ass pupils. My eyes narrowed. "Andre, you okay?"

"Yeah." He walked out of the kitchen past the dining room. I followed after him into the living room.

His sister sucked her teeth and marched out of the living room.

"What wrong?" I asked.

"Nothing. You ready to eat?"

"I guess. But shouldn't we wait for your other guests?"

"They said they'd be running a little behind and to start without them. Come on. Sit down and I'll serve you."

We walked back into the kitchen.

I wondered why he didn't wait for them to arrive. But since I was probably going to feel shy in front of them and his sister, anyway, maybe it was better to eat before they came.

I sat down at the table in the dining room, and a few moments later he placed a plastic bowl in front of me with the spaghetti in it and a plastic fork. *What the fuck indeed?*

He sat across from me and winked. Then he hopped up again and left the dining room.

I dug in, expecting to taste ground beef, noodles, and a marinara sauce, but chewed on noodles, tomato sauce, and wieners instead. *This shit is nasty,* I thought. I was struggling to eat it when Andre came back again and took his seat. His sister followed behind him.

She went straight to the stove and fixed herself some of that shit. But instead of joining us, she went into the living room.

He pierced her with a long and hard look for what seemed like five minute but was probably only one.

"Are you gonna eat?" I asked as he continued to mean mug her.

She tossed her eyes his way and munched on that spaghetti like it was filet mignon.

Then Andre hopped up again. "I'll be back, Allure."

Now, I didn't know what the problem was between him and her, why they kept tossing each other looks. But I wondered why he kept going from room to room. I assumed Andre had diarrhea. Poor thing, he must be embarrassed to have that on a date. Why else would he keep running back to the bathroom? And as far as the sweat was concerned, he always sweated. As for his sister and them looks he was casting her, maybe it was because she was being so damn rude. She wouldn't talk to me, and she wouldn't sit with us to eat. If Crystal had behaved that way when I had a dinner guest, I would be giving her mean looks too.

I watched her turn the bowl up and suck the remaining liquid from it into her mouth before rising to her feet and heading past me into the kitchen, up to the stove. She gave herself another helping.

I tried to stir up a conversation with her. "The weather has been crazy, hasn't it?" I asked.

"Terrible." She pierced me with the same look her brother had given her.

I put my head down and stirred my food with my fork, wishing the nasty shit would vanish off of my plate. I didn't want to eat it, but I didn't want to be rude.

"Well, they said it was gonna rain tomorrow."

"Humph." She didn't even bother sitting down. She scarfed the spaghetti down as she stood.

Noodles, cut-up wieners, and sauce dripped from the bowl as she ate. The food dripped on her Nike shirt, her pink leggings, and her dirty-ass feet, which I just now noticed, and onto the floor.

I kept a smile on my face.

Then suddenly she shoved her bowl down on the counter and rushed off again, mumbling, "Muthafucka."

Five more minutes went by, and I didn't see either one of them. *What in the hell is going on, and where in the hell are his other guests?* I thought.

The doorbell rang.

"Andre? Wanda?"

I rose to answer the door. His other "guests" were a weird-looking white dude with a cigarette in his mouth and an even trashier-looking black chick. *What the fuck?*

I stepped back and closed the door, uncomfortable about letting them inside. They opened it right back up and came inside. My heart started beating. This shit was not right.

I went to go find Andre.

I stomped to the back of the house, yelling, "Andre? Andre?" I turned a corner and saw a set of bedrooms. I went inside both of them. Both were empty, *empty* meaning they didn't have no damn furniture in them or Andre or Wanda. I turned another corner. "Andre?" I jumped when I spied his sister leaning against a wall, her eyes closed. "Where Andre?" I demanded.

She pointed an ugly-ass finger at a half-closed door. A sly smile curved on her lips.

I ignored her and raised my fist to knock but dropped it when she said, "He dressed. You can go in. You are his girl, aren't you?" I could have sworn I heard her chuckle.

I cut my eye at her and shoved the door open, and when I saw what I saw, I screamed, more horrified than I had ever been in my life, like I saw a ghost. I backed up and bumped into her. She stumbled but regained her balance, muttering, "Damn."

I backed away, my heart beating faster by the second, and then ran from the hallway to the dining room to snatch up my purse. Then I continued to run! Run! Run!

But I couldn't get the image of what I saw out of my head. Andre was sitting on his toilet, had a crack pipe in his mouth, and was sucking on it. It wasn't a cigarette flavor I had been tasting when I kissed him. It was a crack flavor. And all the sweating was from the crack! Why the fuck hadn't I figured it out? Stupid! Stupid Stupid! This was why he didn't have much furniture, and come to think of it, this was why he always drove his patrol car. He probably didn't have a car.

My feet wouldn't stop moving. I ran out the front door. Just in case he came outside, I jogged in place at my vehicle until my shaking hands were able to unlock it. At least my legs and feet would still be in motion.

But he didn't.

The sister did, though. After I had hopped in, closed and locked my door—I didn't bother with my seat belt— and started my ignition. I busted a quick U-turn and looked in my rearview mirror. She waved at my car and smiled as I sped down the street. It was the first smile I had gotten out of her ass all night.

"You're back early," my sister commented when I arrived home.

I didn't say shit, just asked, "Where is Sierra?"

"Still asleep. Why?" She inspected my face. "What's wrong?"

"Nothing." I tossed my purse next to her on the couch. Then I slid down to the carpet, staring off into space.

My sister was silent.

How could I have been so blind as not to see that I had been dating a crackhead? I started laughing. At first it was a quick chuckle; then it got louder, came from my belly. I clutched it and tossed my head back, slapped my thighs with my free hand.

"Allure?"

My laughter got louder. I rolled on my belly and continued to clutch it. Then my fists pounded on the carpet, because I was no longer laughing. Now I was screaming. "Allure!"

Then, when my hands became sore, I covered my face and bawled like a baby, worse than Sierra when she thought she was Tony Hawk and tried to ride her skateboard off the porch and landed on her leg, sustaining a superlong gash that left a scar.

I felt my sister's arms around me. I was so tired of getting my hopes up and finding out that each man was a fucking train wreck. Something was clearly wrong. Maybe I was meant to be alone and I needed to take a break from dating. Each guy I had gotten involved with, I should not have. I also thought that because of my situation with James, I was vulnerable. For one, I was not completely over him and the breakup was only a few months ago and I was still hurt. I had known from the beginning, before I started seeing Andre or Bryce, that I should stay my ass alone. And it didn't work with either of them. I should have listened to my mama and that logical voice in my head.

I thought about Andre's ass. Again, I asked myself how I could not have known this man was a damn crackhead. Was him inviting me to dinner like a coming-out party? I needed to forget about it. I knew that what was done was done. I had to pick up the pieces and move on. More importantly, I was glad I had found out about him and Bryce when I did, and not later. That was the good part about both situations.

Chapter 24

When it rains, it pours. My baby girl, my 1994 baby blue Honda Civic, gave out on me today. Since my sister spent the night with my black ass in my distraught state, she offered to take Sierra to the babysitter and pick her up for me. I called my boss and told her I wouldn't be going to work today so I could see about my car. I was going to wait for my mechanic's shop to open and have it towed there. I hoped it wouldn't be too expensive to fix. I put on my cheerful smile and dressed Sierra in a pink jumper and put her thick hair in two puff balls. I ate cereal with her. I didn't much taste mine but acted like it was the best damn bowl of cereal I had ever had, 'cause Sierra had poured it in the bowl for me and I wanted her to enjoy hers. When we finished, I gave her a big kiss, then watched Crystal and her leave.

A few minutes later I jumped in the shower, hoping to shake my somber mood, but couldn't. I had soaped up and was rinsing off when I heard somebody knocking on my door.

With all that had happened, from Bryce and me to Andre being a drug addict, I freaked out. "Goddamn it, what is it now! Is some fucking body going to kill me?" I yelled, flinging my arms. I felt like I was going crazy. I quickly rinsed the rest of the soap off of me, hopped out, wiped the water off my face, blinked, then pulled on my bathrobe.

But I didn't go to no damn door. I grabbed my cord-less and peered out the window, just in case it was a damn lunatic. I had several on my list to choose from. I figured I could call the police.

When I discovered who it was, my heartbeat slowed down, because it wasn't Greg, Bryce, or Andre. It was James.

I didn't feel fear when I saw him, but more of a long-ing.

I smoothed my hair back. It didn't look too bad, since I had had it freshly done for the dinner/crack party with Andre. I took a deep breath, opened the door slowly, and stared at him.

He struggled with his mouth, like he didn't know whether to smile or frown at me, or at himself maybe.

I didn't do either, just clasped my hands behind my back and looked at him with a quizzical expression that translated as "What the hell do you want?" Instantly, I wondered why he was at my doorstep and what he could possibly say after leaving Sierra and me, like we didn't mean anything to him, when we were going through something as well. James wasn't the only one hurt by Jeremiah's death. But James couldn't see past his own pain. He was selfish.

He finally smiled at me, and he shoved his hands into his slacks.

I bit my bottom lip.

Still no words from either of us.

It felt awkward.

I cleared my throat and scratched my scalp, careful not to mess up my hair.

He coughed.

I broke the silence. "Why are you here?"

He curved an arm around my waist and gently moved me from the doorway and strolled inside like he owned the place. He had always been a cocky motherfucker.

Before, I never stopped him, and I didn't stop him now. Because I still loved him.

We didn't even sit, just faced each other. It reminded me of that time he came over to confront me about Greg, how he was on a mission to get me. My, had things changed since then.

I stared into his smoky brown eyes and repeated my question. "You still haven't answered my question, James. Why are you here?"

He stepped closer to me, grabbed my chin in his right palm, lifted my face, studied it. He saw the scar in the corner of my mouth, where Bryce had slapped me. The scar left by my wound that needed stitches. I knew it would never fade and would serve as a memory of that night. I still remembered the pain of his ring slicing into my flesh.

"How did you get this?"

I shook my head and tried to push his hand away. I didn't wanna talk about that night ever.

The grip on my chin tightened.

"Did that muthafucka do this to you?"

I knew he was asking about Greg.

I shook my head. "No, he didn't, and I don't want to talk about it."

He frowned like he wanted to press the issue. But he said instead, "Okay. It don't take away from nothing, Allure. You're still beautiful, baby. You always will be."

I didn't say anything to that.

Then he reached over and kissed the scar gently, making my heart flutter, because it felt like old times.

His lips slid over and found mine, and he kissed me again.

At first, I didn't respond, but he moved in on me, invaded my space by stepping between my legs and holding my waist. He started nipping on my bottom lip, pecking the top, sliding his tongue around my teeth, my tongue. He started rubbing on my body. My terry-cloth robe seemed invisible. I could feel the heat of his fingers like I was completely naked. His hand grabbed my butt; then his fingertips glided up and down my thighs. He kissed me on my neck until I moaned. His hands groped my breasts and teased my nipples.

I put my hands on his cheeks, pulled his face down to me for a kiss.

I allowed him to open my robe, let him back me into the living room wall. He crouched down, pulled my thighs apart, spread my pussy lips, and kissed my pussy like he had my mouth. Wetting his lips with his tongue, he kissed it again, creating that same heat his tongue would have. I moaned and clenched my hands over his waves. He flicked his tongue around my pussy lips, smoothed my juices with his finger, allowed my lips to get real wet, shiny, creamy with my cum, and then licked it all off. His finger stroked deep inside me, one, then two, while his mouth sucked on my clit. His fingers did a quick movement, and I felt like I was going to pee on myself, but instead cum seeped out of me and dripped on my thighs.

James rose to his feet, wrapped my legs around his waist, lifted me, and carried me just like that into the bedroom. He laid me on the bed and swiftly stripped out of his clothes. He played with my naked body some more, touching my hard nipples, putting his mouth on them, flicking his fingers across them, and looked at the expression I gave with each move. He kissed on my tummy, lifted each of my thighs and tongue kissed them, slid my feet one by one to his mouth, sucked on my toes. He then pulled my thighs apart farther and slid between them. He unwrapped a condom, slid it on, then, while watching me, positioned himself at my pussy.

"Put it in, Allure."

I sat up in the bed, put my hands between his legs, gripped his hard dick, and put it at my opening. He had his eyes closed as inch by inch I pushed it into my pussy. Once it was in completely, he gasped loudly and pulled it out. I curved my thighs and held them at his waist. He looked down at me and dived back in, using the strength in his legs to go as deep as he could into me.

"Ooh, James," I moaned.

"I know, baby."

He lowered his head and started kissing me with the same intensity as before, sucking my lips, slamming into my teeth, teasing me all over, tracing my scar with his tongue, then licking back and forth over my nipples till they were glossy with his saliva. He pumped again with a steady rhythm, not fast, though, trying to get it in as deep as he could again.

He sucked on my neck, gripped my breasts tightly in his hands.

He went faster. I felt myself shaking underneath him, had a hard time holding my legs up now. He grasped them in his hands, leaned down and kissed my thighs again, came through again with smooth strokes, looked down at my glassy eyes as ecstasy took over me, leaned back down and kissed me, swallowing my scream. He started to growl and pump faster. I felt his hands tighten on my thighs. He growled louder, more fiercely, and his kiss was rougher again, and that was when he came.

James held me afterward. Which was cool. It felt good. But I couldn't just keep silent about the situation. I hadn't seen him in four months, and he just popped up? I had to know some things, so I said, "James."

"Yes, baby?" He kissed me on my forehead.

"What are we doing here?" There were other things I wanted to ask him like, "Where you been? Why'd you leave? Do you miss us? Do you know how much we miss you? Will you come back? Will you love us again please?"

He took a deep breath and hugged me tighter. "Look, Allure, I love you and never stopped, despite all this time that has passed. But you and I both know that there is a lot we need to discuss." He chuckled. "To tell the truth, baby, I hadn't planned on doing this, but you know what you do to me when I get around you. And you looked sexy with that robe on." He kissed my bared back and slid out of the bed.

I turned over on my side and watched him dress.

"I need to run to the office real quick and finish up the time cards before my boss writes me up," he explained. "That shouldn't take me no more than twenty minutes to do. Just gotta make the copies and drop them in my sup's mailbox. Then I'll come right back, and we can discuss us, Allure, and just what we're gonna do about us."

Chapter 25

That gave me hope that all of this shit that had happened over the past four months wasn't just for me to cry and hurt. It was for a reason. To unite James and me. Maybe God's plan was for me, James, and Sierra to be a family. Maybe, eventually, we could also work on having another baby. I knew that if he let me this time around, I could help him get past the death of our son. I knew the sadness would always be there. But I knew that if he would just talk to me about it, the pain would get better. Because our struggle with it was the same.

I smiled and took a deep breath.

James winked at me.

My eyes went to the crib. Still hadn't got rid of it. Couldn't.

I ran a hand over my hair. The curls had fallen, so it hung silkily around my face.

He adjusted his tie quickly and watched me. "You look pretty with your hair like that, babe."

I blushed. "Thanks, James."

He slipped into his shoes.

I rose and snatched the sheet up, wrapped it around myself so I could follow him to the door. He curled an arm around my waist and my head rested on his shoulder as we walked. Once we made it to the door, he turned back around and slipped his arm from around my waist. When he pulled away, he had this weird look in his eyes. He kissed me so gently and then got a little rough with me. Our teeth bumped into each other, and he nicked my bottom lip, smashed my nose with his lips, so I laughed and shoved him away. But he went for my lips again. I let him; then he pulled away.

"Allure, remember what I said. I love you."

I smiled and stroked his cheek. "I love you, too, baby. Always have."

With that he walked down the steps.

I went into my bathroom and took a quick shower. I was so happy that James was coming back to talk about us. I also knew that Sierra would be so excited if James came back.

I finished showering, rubbed myself down with the lotion James loved. It was the Sun-Ripened Raspberry Body Lotion from Bath & Body Works, mixed with baby oil. I sprayed on some perfume and threw on a summer dress and some flip-flops. I pinned the front of my hair up and even put on a little lip gloss. I hoped he would stay awhile and would have dinner too.

I went into the kitchen and pulled out some steaks. I put the steaks in the sink and turned on the cold water so they would thaw. I then went into Sierra's room and cleaned it up. When the tow truck came and picked up my car, I didn't bother going with the driver to the car repair shop. I didn't want to miss James when he came back. Once the driver had my car loaded on the tow truck, I gave him the shop's address, dashed back inside, and called my mechanic and told him to call me back once he figured out what the problem was.

Hours passed and James still hadn't come back or called.

My sister brought Sierra home, and my mechanic finally called and said that I needed a new engine for my car. I didn't even try to figure out how I was going to pay for it.

All my mind was on was James and when he was coming back.

As planned, I put the steaks on, wrapped some potatoes in foil, placed them in the oven to cook, and pulled up to the table to help Sierra with her homework. Although my mind was not completely on it, I did the best I could. Every two minutes I was staring at the clock or waiting to hear the phone ring.

As soon as Sierra had read her book to me for the ten minutes I'd allotted, I watched her shove her things into her backpack. She ran for the door, screaming, "I'm going to play with my friend outside, Mommy!"

That left me at that table, twiddling my thumbs, wondering where James was, why he hadn't called or come back like he said he would, wondering why, when I called his cell phone, it said the number wasn't in service. This situation had me up and wondering all night, because he never showed, never called, never answered his phone when I dialed his number.

I was down. I felt defeated. I pulled out the bottle of gin I kept way, way back in the cupboard for situations like this, when sleep wouldn't come and the ache wouldn't go away. I just wanted to feel numb. No stress, no worries. I wanted to stop asking myself, *What's wrong with me? Am I unlovable? What did I do wrong? If I look this way . . . acted this way . . . will things change? Or is this gonna be how it's gonna be?* See, it was not that I just had to be with somebody. It was not that simple. The problem was that *not* being with someone hurt so damn much.

Loneness was some cold shit. I had never anticipated that it would feel the way it did. It was almost like when I came in my house, I felt cold air embracing me, 'cause there was no one to come home to and no one to come home to me. Sometimes I almost didn't want to come home. I dreaded it. It harbored the utter loneness I felt when I was out and about with Sierra and saw couples. With no one on my arm, I felt like a dumb ass at family events. I had no one to wrap their arms around me at night. All those things were bad, but it was not even that. It was just the feeling of the void. The void was killing me. Never, ever had I thought that the hardest thing in my life would be finding somebody to love me. Why was that shit so hard?

I continued to sip on the gin and cry. It was so nasty, but it was doing what it needed to. I thought, *Keep me single for the rest of my life . . . cool, but take away that horrible feeling that it gives me. Make the thought of not being with someone mundane, make me voluntarily stoic, and I'll be cool.* I mixed the gin with some lemonade to make it taste a little better. When half the bottle was gone, I pushed it away and lay down in my bed. All it really did in the end was make me sleep better and make my stomach hurt.

But the shit for sure gave me a headache in the morning. One of the reasons I didn't drink was that it made me nauseous and gave me an aching head. This usually overrode my desire to get drunk.

"Mommy? Mommy?"

Sierra was shaking me. I opened my eyes. They were barely slits.

"Mommy, did you forget I gotta go to La La's today? The teacher is coming, and we are going to put on a play. I need to go, Mommy." She was jumping up and down eagerly.

I rubbed my eyes and groaned, "No. I just overslept."

"Ooh, Mommy, your breath stanks!" she exclaimed, giggling and holding her nose.

I gave her the tongue, then sat up, took a deep breath, and swung my legs to the carpet.

"Mommy, I'm gonna wear this, okay?"

For the first time I noticed what Sierra was wearing. Sierra had grabbed some silly shit to put on. Different material, different colors, different socks, different shoes. She had mixed summer and winter clothes, classical dress and eclectic. She had on some sweats and a poncho, rain boots, and wore a choker around her neck. To top it all off, she had done her hair too. Globs of grease were in her curly mane, and barrettes were hanging off the tips of her uncombed hair. *Oh Lord.*

I shrugged. She was only four, so I didn't think it would hurt. Sierra always looked really nice.

"Yeah, let me call your aunt. She can take you."

I grabbed my cell phone. James hadn't called. I dialed my sister's number and asked her to drop Sierra off at school and me at work. I would just stay on campus during my break after work and go to my classes.

"Look, Auntie Crystal. I dressed myself!" Sierra explained as she got in my sister's truck.

"I see." My sister turned to me and lowered her voice. "What the fuck is she wearing?"

I shook my head and offered no reply.

After we dropped Sierra off, my sister set off for my school. However, I knew I wouldn't be able to function or even concentrate until I talked to James.

So I told my sister to turn around and hit the 91 Freeway.

She did and gave me a curious look. "Where am I taking you?"

"To see James."

"James? Why?"

"I don't want to talk about it. Just take me please."

"Okay."

And we headed out to Baldwin Hills.

A little while later I took a deep breath as I sat in my sister's truck outside the house James shared with his brother. I could not believe he would do me like this.

His ass owed me an explanation for all the shit he had done to me. *How the fuck are you going to pop back in my life, make a promise to me, and bounce and not come back? Hell no,* I thought.

"You need me to go with you?" my sister asked.

"No. I'm good."

I got out of the truck, closed the door, and marched up the steps. I rang the doorbell and waited. Nothing. I rang it again. Nothing yet again. His fucking truck was parked in the driveway, so he had to be here! And if a bitch was there, oh well! He didn't have to be to work until ten.

I knocked, rang the doorbell, rang the doorbell again, knocked, and called out his name. "James! James!" I shouted. I had broken into a sweat. My knuckles and the sides of my hands were red, and still I heard and saw no one. *He has to be hiding inside like a bitch,* I thought.

I pounded on the door, ignoring the sting. "James!" Nothing.

"You bastard!" I yelled. I banged some more. I screamed his name till I had a dry mouth.

And still he wouldn't come outside.

I turned my back, defeated, took a deep breath, and was a step away from the door, heading toward my sister's truck, when I heard the lock click and the door slide open.

I spun around quickly.

But it wasn't James. It was his brother, the one who showed up at church when Jeremiah got baptized, the one who came to scoop James up so they could go play some b-ball, and the one who was looking at me like I was the most pathetic thing that ever cursed the earth.

"Where is James?" I placed my hands on my hips, met his gaze.

He was silent.

Fuck it. I rushed up the steps and tried to brush past him. He blocked my way.

"Excuse me," I said.

"Allure."

"What?"

He looked me in my eyes and said firmly, "James is not here."

"I'm not stupid." I pointed at James's truck and bulged my eyes at him and cocked my head to the side. "Now, let me in."

"No."

"Yes."

"Look, girl, you need to go home."

"I'm not going no damn where."

He brought his brows together, like I was crazy. "What is wrong with you?"

"Don't worry about it."

He grabbed my shoulders and tried to press me backward. I wouldn't budge. "You gonna get off my property."

"No, you gonna get out my way. Look, I need to talk to James. He's gonna give me an explanation for why he did what he did to me. Why he left me after Jeremiah died. Why he came to my house, fucked me, and never came back, but promised to come back. He's gonna tell me why he loves me if he seeks to hurt me. He's gonna tell me like a man should!"

"He not here."

"Bullshit!"

He raised his voice. "Look, Allure, go home!"

"No! Not until I talk to James."

"The information you want, you can't get now."

"Why?"

"'Cause he ain't fucking here!"

"Well, where in the fuck is he?"

"On a plane, on the way to his honeymoon. James got married yesterday."

Some things needed to be repeated. This was a case in point. "What?" I said to James's brother.

He repeated, "James got married yesterday, Allure. I'm sorry to . . ." Blah, blah, blah . . . I was too busy holding my shattered face in my hands to listen.

I felt like I was walking on broken glass, barefoot, when I made my way to my sister's truck, because each step hurt. I told myself I wasn't gonna cry in front of his brother, who watched me like I was a movie. I managed to get in the car and close the door, and I just sat there and cried and cried and cried.

I ignored my sister, who kept asking me what was wrong. But then I threw myself in her arms. I felt my shoulders racking, and I had a hard time breathing, because his words didn't hurt me. They killed me.

Chapter 26

They say that you never really know a person and that time doesn't make a friend. Some people even say that there are always signs that something is bound not to work out. That was all true sometimes, but usually it was not so simple. My logic was, number one, a person showed you what they wanted you to see, and number two, some people just changed over time. So you didn't always have an indication as to how things were gonna turn out till they actually turned out. You couldn't meet a man and determine if he was gonna be the greatest love of your lifetime or if he was gonna be the greatest mistake you ever made. Gamble, gamble, gamble that was what love was. And most of all, you couldn't control the motives or actions of others. But when it was revealed . . . Those motives, those actions . . . Then what?

I had to understand this and become better acquainted with this notion. I couldn't change the men of my past. I could change only myself and what I accepted. I cried and cried and didn't want to get out of bed, but in the end, I had reasons to wake up in the morning, and they included Sierra. So I had to clean my face off. I didn't look at Sierra as an obligation. She was a blessing, and my responsibility was ultimately to her. No matter how hard James's betrayal was to face, I had to face it, grieve, and move on from the whole situation. I had no other choice in dealing with the matter.

The last thing I remembered about that day was James's brother, Omar, walking to the car and handing me the itinerary for James's wedding. I saw a picture of James and a woman. It was the chick who was in his car that day. Maybe she had the bomb. Who knows? For a second I thought maybe she had something over me. But I knew better than to second-guess myself given who James chose to deal with. I still had to love myself in spite of all that. So I took my sister's advice and kept busy.

I didn't have my car, but I was able to do what I needed to do by bus. But a car was more convenient. I knew it was only a matter of time before I got another one. I was officially in my last year of college and was doing well in my classes. My hard work, twenty hours a week, earned me a promotion at my school. I was no longer on work study but was a regular school employee. It was only a fifty-cent raise, nothing substantial, but it made me feel good when they acknowledged all the hard work I had been putting in. Any downtime outside of Sierra, work, school, and household duties I put into working out at home. When Sierra went to sleep, I put my iPod on full blast and danced until I sweat. I started getting compliments from people at work and in my classes, and even from random men on the street.

"You looking good, girl!"

I blushed at some dude who was driving by in a shiny blue Caprice Sierra. Sierra and I crossed the street to our home. I had on a pair of jeans and a tank top. I was whipping my body into shape. It was amazing what two months of working out could do to a sista.

He was fine. But, hey, I wasn't ready. I knew I need to take a break and stop jumping from one man to the next out of loneliness. I needed to chill on that.

"Thanks," I told him, acknowledging his compliment when I saw he had stopped his car.

He smiled at me, hesitated, then drove away.

I was glad that he did. I didn't need nothing else to get over. Not now.

When Sierra and I were both inside the gate, I went to my mailbox. Etta was chilling on my stoop, puffing on a cigarette.

"Hey, Etta," I said.

"Hey, girl. Hey, baby." When Sierra made it to our steps, Etta gave Sierra's bottom a pat.

"Hi," Sierra chirped.

"Tired?" I asked, shuffling through the mail I'd retrieved from my mailbox.

"Girl, yes. These white folks gonna kill me one day."

I laughed. "Rest as long as you want. I got some water and juice in here if you want it."

"All right, babe."

I walked past her, unlocked the door, ushered Sierra out of my way, and checked my voice mail. I dialed the number and put in my pass code.

"Mommy, I'm hungry."

"Okay, just a sec, Si."

I cradled the phone to my ear and searched in the fridge for something to feed her. I didn't have time to really cook, because I had a final to study for. "What do you want, Ma? A corn dog or a potpie?"

She put her hand to her little face, like she watched me do when I was thinking. I chuckled and shook my head.

"Umm, potpie," she said.

"You have two new messages," the automated voice said.

I popped the potpie into the microwave, set it at five minutes, and pressed ONE on the phone to hear the first message.

"First message, sent at six forty-five P.M."

"Bitch, where the fuck are you? Lose a few pounds and lose your mind, but you ain't as fine as me."

I love you, too, Creole, I thought and erased the message.

Sierra sat down at the table, fork in hand.

"You're really hungry, aren't you?"

"Yep."

"Okay," I said, smiling. "It will be done in five minutes."

"'Kay. Mommy."

I listened to the next message. "Sent at six fifty-nine p.m."

"Hey, it's me. I know you don't want to hear from me, but I wanted to tell you how sorry I am for the pain I know I've caused you. I shouldn't have come to you that day, Allure, but I couldn't stay away. You have something that I can't get out of my system. And I know this doesn't make a difference, but, baby, I do care about you. I love you, Allure. I was just calling to say I'm sorry, baby. I never meant to hurt you." The line beeped while he was still talking.

It was James.

I played the message over.

And over.

And over.

I would have played it again if I didn't hear, "Mommy, Mommy."

"Huh?"

"My food's done."

I took the potpie out of the microwave and laid it on the counter to cool, feeling perplexed, not knowing what to say. . . .

***

I got two more disturbing calls at work the next day, when all I wanted to do was watch these people's kids so I could go home to mine. One was from Greg. Greg tried out his new role of a person who had changed and wanted me back, and said that he had gotten baptized and had prayed that God would reunite us and God always answered prayers and blah, blah, fucking blah. But the annoyance in my voice told him I wasn't trying to hear it. The next phone call was from James.

"This is Allure."

Silence.

"This is Allure," I repeated.

"Hi."

I froze. "Who is this?"

"It's James."

I greeted him with silence, which lasted ten seconds before I huffed out hatefully, "Why are you calling me?" I knew I should have hung up on James, like I had on Greg. But truthfully, I wanted to hear what he had to say. I needed to understand why he did me the way that he had.

"Did you get my message?"

"Yes, I did."

"Well, what do you think?"

"Look, James, I don't have time for this, and I really don't know why you're calling me. You have a wife, remember? Someone you loved enough to marry."

"No, I love you."

"What?"

"Baby, I'm sorry. I didn't know things were going to be this way. I can't stop thinking about you. I didn't know things were going to end up like this."

I breathed deeply into the phone. *He loves me, but he married someone else?* I thought.

"Baby, I'm so sorry."

"James, please."

"Baby, let me make this right. Let's meet so we can talk."

"No!"

"Allure, please, just over lunch. I can't move forward until I make this right with you, baby," he pleaded.

"James, I don't think I should see you."

"Just lunch. I promise. We can meet somewhere, talk, and then I'll leave you alone. Allure, I swear to God."

Truth was, I wanted to hear what he had to say. Maybe hear an apology and an explanation. That would take the anger away, so I could get over him fully, forgive him. Forgiving really was not so much about, "Okay, I forgive you for doing bad." It was more about letting go of the hope that things could be different than they were. I needed to do that with James.

"All right, all right, but lunch and that's it."

"Okay, you name when and where."

"Tony's on the Pier. Saturday. At one p.m."

"I'll be there, baby."

Chapter 27

I borrowed my sister's truck to go see James. When I made it to the restaurant, James was already seated and looking at a menu. I watched him for a couple of seconds before making my way over to him. He smiled and stood to his feet. When he tried to embrace me, I took a step back.

Embarrassed, he said, "Let me get your chair for you, baby."

"Thank you."

He eyed me up and down as I lowered myself to my seat.

"You look nice. I never saw you wear that dress before."

I gave him a cold stare. Then I looked down at my black dress and pumps. The dress was short sleeved, tight fitting, and I was wearing the hell out of it. Thanks to my nightly workouts, my waist had gone in, my booty was poking out, and my calves were banging. I had my little Jeremiah to thank for my rump. I had James drooling. He wouldn't stop his eyes from flickering down my body. Maybe he couldn't. *Humph. Humph. Humph.*

"Thanks. It was a gift from my sister. She bought it for me, hoping it would make me feel better."

Stupidly he asked, "Better about what?"

"You leaving," I replied sharply. "Coming back, making passionate love to me, promising to come back to me, leaving, not coming back, and then, without informing me, getting married."

He took a sharp intake of breath and looked down. "Man . . . I deserve that."

"Yeah, you *really* do."

There was silence as we looked at our menus. While I looked at mine, I could feel James studying me.

James broke the silence by saying, "I ordered you a pink lemonade, baby."

I ignored the comment and continued to look at my menu.

A few minutes later the waitress, a friendly blond girl, came to our table. "Hello. I'm Rachel. I'll be your server. Would you guys like to order now?"

Without hesitation James said, "Steak, well done, and a loaded baked potato."

She jotted it down. "Okay, and for you, miss?"

Without even glancing at the menu, I said, "The filet mignon, with a side of jumbo shrimp, a Caesar salad, and two petite lobster tails. Oh, and a side of crab legs."

James didn't even so much as glance my way for ordering all that food—which I had no intention of eating, but since it was the last time he would be able to take me out to eat, I was going to make his ass come out the pocket. However, the waitress did.

I gave her a sharp look that faded her shocked expression. "Problem, Rachel?"

She smiled and gushed out, "No, no, I'll go put in your order." She collected the menus and walked back to the kitchen.

Once she was gone, James turned back to me. "It's so good to see you, Allure."

***

He tried to touch my hand, which lay flat on the table, but I pulled it away and clasped both my hands on my lap.

He looked hurt at my coldness and said, "I know you're mad at me. But you gotta understand that I didn't want things to be this way? I wanted to be with you. I still want to."

"You have a wife now, dum-dum!"

I looked pointedly at the shiny ring that glistened on his left hand. What was wrong with him? Did he forget that he had made a vow before God? Now it appeared he was trying to break the shit.

"But she's not the one I want."

What? No! I wasn't going to fall for that, so I kept my poker face.

"Look, she was pregnant. That's why I married her. I didn't want to do her dirty."

He got me with that one. The pain made me unable to swallow for a second. But I tried to stay strong. I didn't want him to see me break down. "So was I," I whispered. "I gave you a child. It didn't stop you from doing me dirty."

"Yeah, well, he's dead. Get over him."

Low.

"How the fuck could you?" That was what my look said. Then the callous mention of our son caused tears to spill from my eyes.

"No, I didn't mean that. Listen. She started out as a sidepiece. She knew her position, and she was with it. Then I realized she was better for me. We're on the same level, she has no kids, no baggage from a past re-lationship, and she is already established. She has her own place, and it's not in the *hood*. She has a house.

She comes from a good family. She's been finely bred. She's a Zeta, has her master's and whatnot and . . ." He coughed. Then he looked down at the table. He took a sip of his water.

He'd avoided my eyes while he said what he said. He'd made it seem like it was my fault he made the decisions he made. Why did he continue to hurt me? It would have been better if he had just plain out said, "I love her. I never loved you."

I wanted to say, "Yeah, she's fucking fabulous, but the bitch knew you had a woman and she was content with you giving her head in your truck?"

"What the fuck does this have to do with how you did me?" I said instead.

His lips popped out. He looked irritated. "I'm trying to say sorry. Why can't you just . . . just . . ."

"Just what?"

"Stop being bitter, Allure."

"I'm not bitter I'm hurt, and I'm tired. Tired of men like you who dump their issues on women like me."

"Yeah, and what kind of woman are you, Allure?"

"A damn good fucking one with a lot of potential, even if you didn't see it. One who can go through shit and hurt so much, where it feel like I've died, like I've lost a piece of who I am as a woman. And even after all of this, I still find a reason to wake up and smile. I'm somebody that loves so damn hard and so damn good. Ain't shit about me watered down. You got the best I had. And men like you wanna rob me of that best, which should be reserved for a man worthy of it.

"You pretend to be that man. Then, when he do come, I ain't got nothing to give him, because by the time I get to him, sorry-ass men like you have drained me. I tell you, it fucks me up because you don't want to share with me that you don't wanna do right. So you pretend to do right, while all along, behind my back, you doing me so wrong. Like I asked you to be there. I didn't. And finally, I'm tired of men like you who come into my life, reserve your spot in my baby's heart, and walk out of it, and it's so fucking easy. Like this thing . . . life is all about you and don't nobody else matter."

I got closer to his face. "You came in my life, and you fought for me. Said you would never play me like other men would. You ended up hurting me more than anyone could. I gave you what you wanted, and I never half stepped. I didn't come with the problems I could have come with, James. I loved you, really loved you. When I told you I was pregnant, you was cool on me. Fine. I went on. Then here you come again. But you still had no real intent to do right. If you did, you wouldn't have been fucking around.

"Then I take you back, and when we needed each other the most, you bounced. You pop back up, fuck me, and leave. And if that's not enough, you slap me in the face by getting married and explaining how she is more of a woman for you and how I'm not! Bullshit. You don't want me, cool. But don't come back, make promises, and leave me again. You don't love me, cool, but don't you dare sit in my face and hold me responsible for that! Try to make me feel like I'm lacking something, 'cause you ain't shit and 'cause you lack a conscience and fucking humility."

He placed one of his hands in the air. "Okay, you're right, Allure. I know I fucked up. And I know what kind of woman you are. I know you're a good woman baby. But I really thought I didn't want to be with you. I popped back up to tell you I was getting married. And truth be told, I realized in that moment, standing in your living room, that you were the one I loved, not her, and that I craved for time to rewind and that day I treated you the way I did that I had did things differently, held you, comforted you, and made love to you again. Went to sleep in your arms, then woke up, fed Sierra, went on to work, and looked forward to being in your arms when I came home. But it was too late, and I couldn't do shit about it but make love to you and marry my fiancée.

"Somewhere along the way the wrong things became important to me. So my mind was already made up. But in that moment, staring at you in that robe, seeing that look you had in your eyes, the way you used to stare at me, Allure, like I was a king, same with Sierra . . . Being around you two . . . baby, it was different than with any other woman. I always felt like I was important. Doing simple shit, like dumping the trash, you were always gracious, appreciated me. If I brought Sierra a lollipop, you would have thought I delivered a fucking pony on your doorstep."

He went on. "And, shit, I felt powerful with you, like a real man. You let me lead, and you respected the decisions I made. You let me have it however I wanted it whenever I wanted it. You made a point to please me. You engaged with me. Listened to all the bullshit I talked like you were really interested. You wanted me there. I felt like I had a real woman that would do anything for me and would always be loyal to me.

"Jeremiah's death crushed me. I wouldn't grieve. Instead, I filled myself up with anger and took it out on you, when, baby, I know you were hurting just as much as I was. And even in your pain you tried to help me get past mine. How could I not have loved a woman like you? That's how you used to make me feel, and when I went back that day to see you, you still had that look, still after all I had done. It showed me you could love me again . . . showed me you still loved me. She and I . . . . it doesn't feel like it feels when it's you and me together."

The stuff he was saying was crushing me. Because he did love me, and if he had done some things different, we would still be together. And he had completely ruined the chance of mending our relationship by marrying her. He didn't have to do that!

"If you felt that way, then why didn't you call the wedding off? Why leave me with a false pretense and go off and marry someone else?"

"At the time I thought it was the right thing to do because she was pregnant."

"Okay. So you have a wife and a baby on the way with this *better* woman, right? Then what do you want from me?" I was trying hard to look at him, but his words had me teary-eyed, so I kept my eyes closed. I loved him and I couldn't . . . I couldn't have him.

"I want to see you again, baby. I can't divorce her. But I can't not have you in my life."

No, the fuck he didn't! See me again? That was what this was about? He was trying to fuck around on his wife with me, and he thought I was going to let him? He had me fucked up. As much as I loved him and probably would always love him, I refused to be a sidepiece.

"No." I grabbed my purse and stood to my feet.

He stood as well.

"You know what? I knew you didn't invite me here to *make things right*. I shouldn't have even agreed to meet you. After all we have shared, gone through, and all you have done to me, you want to make me a sidepiece."

"Allure!"

"Look, you had my trust and my love. I begged you not to hurt me, to be up front, and you weren't. You came into my and Sierra's life, and you fucked it up. Now we back on track. We've moved past this and you. . . ." I took a deep breath. "Save this. You don't know what the fuck you want. So I'm not gonna entertain your bullshit. I have given you chance after chance, and every damn time that I do, you do some shit to hurt me."

When I say I was crying, man, was I crying.

"Sierra and I, we deserve so much more than you. Somebody who is going to love us, honor us, protect our hearts, not continue to step on them. He will appreciate the blessing that he has. That's something you could have done, but you chose not to."

I turned to go and was walking to the door when he chased after me and grabbed my arm snugly.

"I love you, baby. Don't end it like this." It was like he was warning me.

I looked him squarely in his eyes. "*You* ended it like this. Go home to your ugly-ass wife."

I released his hold on my arm and walked out the door.

My composure during our confrontation vanished as soon as I made it to my sister's truck. For thirty minutes I cried like a baby, for a mixture of reasons. Some I understood; some I didn't. I understood that this was someone I had come to care for deeply. Someone I had made love to, had had a kid with, and someone who had never belonged to me and never would. He had basically tried to change my status. He wanted me to be the jump-off now that she was wifey. And the truth was, I felt sorry for her, because if he hadn't introduced her to heartache yet, he would. Funny thing was, at first, when I found out that he had married another

woman, I wanted to be that woman. Now I wanted neither of those spots. She had actually done me a favor,
because James was now out of my life for good.

Epilogue

May 25, 2011, six months later . . .
I graduated from college. I didn't think I could have got through it or made it this far without a certain day occurring and the encouraging words that day gave me.

It was the day after I had met with James. As much as I knew that I needed to move past him, I was still feeling hurt by the stuff that he told me. I knew I was going to get over this in time. But James and I had a history, so it would not be easy. And to be honest, I thought that the love that I had for him just might be a love that would always be with me.

I was sitting on my porch, watching Sierra play, when Etta's late ass came through the gate. Today she rather quickly deposited the mail in the boxes. I waved at her, and she approached me.

In all the time she had been delivering the mail to our building, Etta had never taken the time to have a heart-to-heart talk with me. We would just say hey and chop it up here and there. But never about personal stuff. But I knew she was nosy as hell and was well acquainted with my business and who came and went from my apartment. So I was surprised when she came over and said, "You mind if I sit next to you?"

"Go ahead."

She got comfortable on the porch. "Thanks, girl. Them white folks ain't gonna kill me today."

I chuckled.

She observed me.

"Did you ever think that the reason you haven't found the right man is because it's not your time? Sometimes God lets bad things happen to us as a sign that something is not right. He also does it to make us stronger. God got a plan for you, and you gotta stop fighting it. I bet that little girl got enough love in her little heart that not ten of these fools you come across could measure up to. And while you out searching, you fail to realize that your time will come, *when it's time*. I'm an old lady, but follow my words, darling. Focus on you, and let God lead that man to you."

Once I got over the surprise of what she had said, I told her, "You gotta excuse my frustration with God, ma'am. Every man he seems to send breaks my heart. All these men I didn't go looking for, and still they managed to hurt me and leave scars."

"Baby girl, them ain't sent from God. God's gonna send you a real *man,* and he's gonna be so good to you that at times you gonna think he's all you need. Damn food, television, the clubs, girlfriends, and jewelry, all that shit. And with everything you give, he's gonna give it right back to you and then some. And when you really look at it, he'll be all you need. And all those clowns from your past will serve their purpose too. They gave you the ability of discernment. So you'll see through the bullshit from this point on. But for now just focus on you and that little girl." She blew a kiss to Sierra. "The right guy, he's gonna love her like she's his own. Why wouldn't anyone, anyway?"

I didn't know what to say, but I didn't get a chance to say anything.

She said, "Girl, go on and get your mail." And she rose and walked toward the gate.

"All right. Come sit with me again sometime," I offered.

She chuckled. "I will."

"Sierra, in a minute you need to come in and help me with dinner."

Although it still sucked to be alone, I had Sierra there with me, so I wasn't so alone. It was just the way I looked at it, I suppose. I didn't have a man by my side, but I had a special little girl who loved me to pieces.

I stood and walked to the mailboxes. I pulled my keys from my wrist and unlocked my mailbox. I knew it wasn't nothing more than bills. I pulled my letters out and closed the box back up. I had my phone bill, gas bill, light bill, cable bill. But there was one more letter peeking through the stack.

"Sierra, come on," I called.

My eyes passed over the label on the last envelope. ACCOUNTABLE HEALTH. My doctor's office. The bastards who let a homeless bitch give me a false reading. What did they want now? I thought. To tell me they had made another mistake and I indeed had AIDS? I ripped open the envelope and yanked out the letter, my fingers rubbing against the staple in it.

Dear Ms. Jones,

I was surprised and disappointed to hear of your unpleasant experience at our facility. Professionalism is important to us, and we strive to provide our patients not only with accurate health services but also with courteous service. Needless to say, we have dealt with this issue internally, and it will never occur again in our facility. Please allow us to fix this problem—so that you don't feel compelled to seek counsel and, more importantly, so we don't lose you as a customer—with this check attached and our sincerest apologies.

I stopped reading the letter and I flipped the page over and my eyes got buckwide. Stapled to the next page was a check for twenty thousand dollars.

I screamed and kicked my feet in the air. That meant I could finish my last year in college without struggling, buy a new car!

Sierra came running up to me. "Mommy, what is it?"

I scooped her in my arms and kissed her all over her face. She laughed and struggled in my arms.

Etta was across the street, watching us and cracking up laughing.

Thinking about that day now had me teary eyed. I looked at where I was then, how hopeless I felt, and how I felt now. I was definitely in better spirits and was so full of hope for the future, for the journey Sierra and I would go on now, and for what God had in store for us.

When the dean of the college announced my name at my graduation, I stood and smoothed down my skirt. I heard my mom, Crystal, Kendra, and Creole. They all screamed my name until their voices sounded strained, but no voice was sweeter than that of my daughter, and when she saw me take the podium, she cheered and clapped with joy. There I was, now twenty-five, a single parent and now a college graduate—the first in my family. I wasn't married, or even engaged, there was no man waiting for me with roses and a kiss, and there was no man to take me out to celebrate my success, a success that seemed to have taken me a lifetime to achieve.

But I was alive, God had got me up that morning, and most of all, I knew I had myself, and that made everything okay. I knew one day God was going to send a man my way, a real man who would love everything about me. But until then I was going to focus on myself and Sierra, like Etta said, and not be so gung ho about giving myself to a man and accepting his BS just to fill the void, just to have a piece of a man. Nor did I need to allow a man to hurt or mistreat me and then just accept it out of fear I would lose that person. I had learned that if a man didn't treat me right, he didn't deserve to be in my life, anyway. I had needed to find a quick-fix-it man and had gone from one bad guy to the next. All that did was bring problems into my life and make it more chaotic. I was moving on and saying good-bye to all that drama.

The End

About the Author

Braya Spice also writes as Karen Williams. She is the author of *Harlem On Lock, The People Vs. Cashmere, Dirty to the Grave, Thug in Me,* and *Aphrodisiacs: Erotic Short Stories.* She is also in the anthologies *Around the Way Girls 7* and *Even Sinners Have Souls Too.* She currently lives in Bellflower, California, works as a probation officer, and is the mother of two, Adara, fourteen, and Bralynn, two.

Notes